CLUB MAFIA – THE BEAST
A DARK MAFIA ROMANCE

STELLA ANDREWS

Copyrighted Material
Copyright © Stella Andrews 2022
Stella Andrews has asserted her rights under the Copyright, Designs and Patents Act 1988 to be identified as the Author of this work.
This book is a work of fiction and except in the case of historical fact, any resemblance to actual persons, living or dead, is purely coincidental.
All rights reserved. No part of this book may be reproduced or transmitted in any form without written permission of the author, except by a reviewer who may quote brief passages for review purposes only.

18+ This book is for Adults only. If you are easily shocked and not a fan of sexual content then move away now.

NEWSLETTER

Sign up to my newsletter and download a free eBook

stellaandrews.com

CLUB MAFIA

THE BEAST

Beasts have sharp claws that draw blood. Sometimes that blood is their own.
When the blood spills and drips through the cracks of insanity a weaker man would curl up and die.

If you're strong you ignore the pain and use it against your enemy.

That man can't fail. That man is now a Beast.

They call me The Beast for a very good reason.

I fight to win and have no fear.

Then I met Winter.

One night only was all we had, but it was a night that changed my life.

They say love can't happen like a bolt of lightning. Lust maybe, but never love.

I disagree.

She was stolen from me and married to another.

I crave any mention of her, and I can't sleep at night worrying about whose arms she lies in. It's the ultimate torture but I am getting used to it. It's woven into the fabric of my life, making me wear the pain.

I will stop at nothing to bring her back to me whether she likes it or not.

She is mine and always will be and this will be the dirtiest fight of my life.

I'm about to start a war.

A Mafia War.

Dark, dangerous, and full of depravity. This book will wrap you in shadows until you can't bear the light. Scenes may upset some readers; you have been warned.

Bleeding romance and suspense, this book ticks all the boxes.

High heat and scenes that are not for the fainthearted.
   If you love a dark Mafia romance, you're in the right place.

PROLOGUE

ALESSANDRO

SICILY

The past two years have been bittersweet because they have been the worst of my life and the best.

Now it's all set to change because the best part of my life will be sacrificed for the one thing I want more than anything. To save Winter and bring her back to us.

I would say, back to me, but we never really got started. One night only was all we had, but it was a night that changed my life.

They say love can't happen like a bolt of lightning. Lust maybe, but never love. I disagree. I love Winter with all my heart because I've never got over losing her and I can't even bear to look at women with similar features. I only employ blondes because they are nothing like my dark, exotic beauty.

I crave any mention of her, and I can't sleep at night worrying about whose arms she lies in. It's the ultimate torture but I'm getting used to it. It's woven into the fabric of my life, making me wear the pain. The only antidote to that was I got to live my dream.

I was set free from a life of madness to step into a different one. Strings were pulled on my behalf, and I found myself directing a movie that won an Oscar fresh off the starting line. I was up and coming and one to watch, and the past two years have been hard in many ways. I rarely sleep and I work too hard to drive away the images of the girl I loved and lost so cruelly.

We have tried so hard to bring her back to us. The plan was shaping up nicely and our positions of power are almost complete. Then Flynn learned our enemy has a daughter, and it changed everything. We thought we had won. We had the golden goose and then Massimo changed the game overnight.

"Buonasera, signor Majerio."

"Buonasera, Tommaso."

I move past the respectful soldier who stands aside to let me pass and let the familiar settle around me like a well-worn cloak.

My grandfather's home. The head office of his Sicilian empire that my own father didn't think he could take on. He fled to Boston and started his own branch of our family, but my grandfather always had me marked as his heir apparent. I was told I reminded him of himself, and he wanted me to leave Rockwell and begin my training. I resisted, and it takes a very foolish person to go against my grandfather, but as it happened, he was feeling generous that day. I was given a respite on the understanding I would take over as the head of this family when he died or was unable to command. I enjoyed two years of freedom, but that has all changed now.

I'm here to take my place by his side for only one reason. To bring Winter home.

The plan was to use my grandfather's connections to back us up and give us a formidable army behind us. It was meant to take place here in Sicily, but Massimo has changed all that and blocked our move.

Now I must convince my grandfather that I know what I'm doing if we are to stand any chance of pulling this off and so as I head into the den where he enjoys a pre-dinner cigar, I set my attitude to bastard.

"Alessandro."

His voice reaches me through the haze of smoke, and I smile when I hear the husky tones of a man who always appears as if he knows everything. I think he does, and my heart quickens when he points to the leather wing-backed chair opposite him and offers me a cigar.

"Brandy and cigars. My guilty pleasure above many others."

His gruff laughter makes me smile and, as I light the tip and take a drag of the pungent smoke, I settle into my role.

Handing me a glass of brandy, he raises his glass to mine. "So, we celebrate."

"We have something to celebrate?"

He laughs softly. "You tell me."

"We will celebrate when Massimo Delauren is dead, Nonno."

"Ah, your greatest enemy."

He puffs on his cigar, appearing in a thoughtful mood, and I wait for him to speak.

"Ma-ss-im-o." He drags out every syllable of his name and I swear every single one of them grates on my nerves.

"He has been tolerated for far too long."

"So, you'll help us."

"You know my price."

"It's why I'm here." I regard him coolly and he nods, apparently satisfied.

"Your first plan has changed, I understand."

"He declined your invitation."

My grandfather sighs heavily.

"An unfortunate response because now we must play Plan B, as they say."

"Which is?"

I'm guessing he has one because he hinted at that and he nods, slowly blowing out the smoke as if he hasn't a care in the world.

I envy him that.

"A good friend of mine has offered to assist with our problem."

"Do I know him?" I'm intrigued, as my grandfather laughs softly.

"Her, Alessandro. Portia Symmons is her name. She runs a modeling agency in Los Angeles close to Massimo's home, well one of them, anyway."

I lean forward as he takes a swig of his drink and sighs happily.

"She was the woman who introduced Massimo to Imogen, his first wife. She modeled for Portia and was the most beautiful woman in LA for many years. She was in great demand, but Massimo fell hard and soon they were married, and she worked no more."

He shakes his head. "The life of a mafia wife is not a free one, and she spent her days closely protected from his many enemies. Sadly, it was Mother Nature who claimed her life, and that is a force Massimo has no control over, no matter how hard he tries."

"So how can she help us?" I'm mystified and my grandfather arches his brow and looks disappointed. "Open your eyes, Alessandro, and look for the opportunity. It helps to understand everything possible about your enemy and I have investigated yours so hard I even discovered how much he weighed when he was born."

I feel foolish because my grandfather is a master of this, and

I must remember that, and he will have everything worked out down to the finest detail.

"They meet once a month at Scarpetta in Beverly Hills. Massimo has a great interest in fashion and adores his monthly conversations with somebody who shares his hobby. Portia is the best at what she does and has several high-profile celebrities among her many clients. Massimo loves to wallow in the shine that glamor provides, and Portia indulges him because he is her biggest benefactor."

He leans forward and I see the evil glint in his eyes as he says softly, "Portia has become increasingly worried about Massimo's state of mind. She senses he's sliding into madness at a breakneck speed. She is no longer comfortable around him and has offered to help us remove him from life."

"Why would she do that? She could be working for him and can't be trusted."

My grandfather merely laughs before taking another lungful of cigar smoke.

"Did I mention she is my mistress?"

For a moment I just stare at him in awe because for fuck's sake, my grandfather must be approaching seventy years old.

He merely winks and clips the cigar and places it back in the box and lifting his glass, he drains it in one huge gulp. I watch the excitement blaze from his eyes as he says with a chuckle, "Just don't tell Nonna, otherwise she'll insist on accompanying me on my next trip there."

I'm not sure how I feel about this because I always thought my grandfather adored his wife, and they were happily married.

He must sense my disapproval because he shrugs. "It's nothing. Just something to make a business trip more pleasurable. Portia knows the score and believe it or not, so does Nonna."

"She knows!"

"Not the details, but she resigned herself to my wandering

eye years ago. When you are in my position, you are faced with a great deal of temptation. It's so easy to have what you want, and it takes a strong man to resist that. Portia is a fine-looking woman who knows how to please a man, and Nonna can't be bothered anymore."

Now I feel nauseous and leaning back in my chair, say with a sigh. "Finish your story."

He laughs at my obvious discomfort and says quickly, "Portia will ask Massimo to bring his wife to the next meeting. She will say she's curious to meet her. We will book every seat in the restaurant and fill them with our men, and one very special diner will arrive with her new husband."

"Charlotte?"

He nods. "We will position her in his view and, using her as a distraction, we will cut the head off the snake."

"It sounds too easy." I think he may have underestimated Massimo and he shrugs. "Sometimes it's better not to overcomplicate things. Massimo won't be expecting an ambush because it's a regular arrangement. While he's dining with his wife and his close friend, you must instruct your friends to use their soldiers and strike his homes, businesses and wipe every trace of Massimo from life."

"This is huge." I'm astonished by the magnitude of my grandfather's plan, and he nods, his lips twisting into the evil grin that earned him his reputation.

"We must go in heavy and leave nothing to chance. Massimo will not leave that restaurant alive. You have my word on that."

He stands and nods toward the door. "It's time to eat and Nonna will be angry if we are late. Come, let us enjoy a family meal and talk about more agreeable things and welcome you home where you belong."

As he slings his arm around my shoulder, it's as if I just

struck a deal with the devil. I have traded my soul and I would do it again in a heartbeat if it brings Winter back to me.

THE NEXT DAY I leave for Club Mafia to inform my friends of the change of plan and to set the wheels in motion of the devastation that will bring Massimo Delauren and his empire to a bitter end. But most of all, it will set Winter free and there is a tiny shred of hope in my heart that she will feel the same and our one night only will turn into the start of something beautiful — for both of us.

CHAPTER 1

WINTER

Massimo appears to be in a good mood today. He gently hums as he works on painting my face like an artist who is happy with his work for once. Many times, he has been irritated with his attempts at creating the perfect masterpiece of flawless perfection. Often, he would scrawl across my face with lipstick as if trying to cover up his mistakes and ending his attempts with an aggressive show of anger.

Today his touch is light, almost gentle, but I don't think the impression of his fingers against my skin will ever stop disgusting me.

His aging face, the deep wrinkles put there by years of savagery and disgusting acts against mankind, outline a living monster who should have been slain centuries ago.

The thinning hair that he so desperately tries to freeze in time, dying it black and undergoing surgery to weave the strands of his victim's hair into his own scalp repulses me. Yes, Massimo is a monster of a unique kind because he plunders their bodies and wears their scalps as a badge of honor. I wonder how many corpses now lie incinerated in his basement, minus their scalps that now live on the head of the man who murdered them.

Sick, twisted, depraved and psychotic. The man who controls every part of me but my soul. That belongs to two men. Three if you count my twin brother Angelo. I endure a living Hell just for them and one day I will slay the monster myself and set us all free.

It's like a wind whipping around my soul, from the ground up. A constant realization that my day creeps ever closer. Something in the air, a faint stirring of destiny that soothes my wearied soul and gently caresses it like a nurturing mother holding their baby. My time is approaching and the man I call my husband will discover what it's like to stare death in the face and know there is no escaping it.

I have heard so many pleas and agonized screams from the many victims he has murdered in the cell next door to my own. I shivered while perched on my swing, waiting for my turn to discover what that feels like. Massimo Delauren is one of Mother Nature's biggest mistakes and when he breathes his last, it will be the most painful experience of his life and my greatest moment.

He leans back and considers his work and I wait for his judgment, fully expecting him to snarl and scream with anger if there is one speck of color out of place or a smudge that renders his art imperfect.

Today he appears happy, and he sings in a childish voice as if he's four years old. *"Pretty, pretty princess, how I love thine beauty. How I love thine smile and how I love thine innocence. Dance with me, my angel, and let thine happiness fill your heart because you belong to me forever until I say otherwise."*

He hums as he pulls me to my feet, and I have no choice but to skip around the dressing room as he twirls me around and laughs like the maniac he is. It's difficult to dance on the high heels he always makes me wear, but I know one false move would sour his good mood in an instant. He may not hurt me physically, but he has damaged my soul with harsh words, cruel acts, and denying me one thing. Access to the one person who keeps my heart beating. My son. Frankie.

As I twirl in the arms of a sadistic horror show, I calm my frantic heart with images of my son. He is the one thing that counts in my life. A gift from God to accompany me through hell and provide a guiding light to walk toward, and I will not fail.

Frankie is growing up and yet I don't get to witness those special milestones first hand. He is locked in his nursery with a faceless nanny, and the only time I visit him is when I have earned the reward. I love it when he smiles up at me from his crib, his long lashes dusting against his cheeks and those beautiful brown eyes filled with innocence and happiness. It's like staring into a duplicate of his father and my heart twists with regret every time I allow myself to let Alessandro back into my head. I try to push him out, to guard my heart against my most treasured memory, but it's always there reminding me how different my life could have been if fate hadn't been so cruel.

One night only was all we had, but what a fucking night it was. We took a moment in the madness and made it ours. A selfish act of greed that erupted into one night of pleasure that I will never forget and not just because of the bundle of both our DNA that rests in his crib upstairs.

For once in my life, I was free. I experienced what it was like to be loved, and Alessandro played that part perfectly. I have come to terms with the fact it was one night only, and I regret nothing. Wherever he is now, whoever he is with, doesn't matter anymore. At least that's what I'm training my heart to believe.

Above all, I hope he's happy and not too disappointed in me because to the outside world I love the monster I call my husband and turned my back on the rest of civilization to live in a gilded cage with him controlling the lock and key.

"Come my darling, today we have a very special treat to enjoy."

My heart sinks when he laughs like the maniac he is. "But first we must visit my wife and Wesley. They will love hearing what I have planned."

The fear creeps across my skin like a case of poison ivy. Just the thought of returning to the mausoleum Massimo has created in this mansion fills me with desperation. Since learning of its existence, I haven't slept out of fear of joining the corpses in the sterile space and I'm nauseous at the thought of spending even just one second breathing the rancid air where death lingers, promising a cruel bitter end.

Massimo is eager to get there it seems and moves at a brisk pace along the marble lined corridor. The place is clean and sterile because any speck of dust sends him into a rage. The servants he employs blend into the surroundings and never appear when he is there. It's as if they fade back into the darkened corners like shadows shrinking from the light.

Once again, he hums as he walks, and I try to still my frantic heart. The last time I met his wife and learned the fate of his friend will be forever etched on my soul as if he took a knife and carved the images into it himself. Dark, cruel, sadistic, and evil. Not really the qualities a woman looks for in a husband and knowing that one day I will end up in that room is enough incentive to make me plot his death a little faster.

As he holds his finger up to the biometric entry system, my heart starts racing with fear and desperation as I consider what the special treat he has lined up could be.

I'm guessing treat is the wrong description entirely because it will probably involve heaping even more misery onto my already burdened shoulders.

As we enter the room, I try not to glance at the golden

effigy spinning above the glass casket, knowing his friend is the only entertainment his dead wife gets to enjoy. Wesley betrayed Massimo and now spins as a golden light above his wife's head as a perpetual punishment for his sins. The fact he's paralyzed and yet lives on inside his mind is almost too much to contemplate and yet knowing how evil Wesley Vasquez was, I can't feel sorry for him. If anything, I'm happy he had the cruelest retribution, which just shows how scarred my mind has become.

"Imogen, my darling, you are looking as beautiful as always."

Massimo falls onto his wife's coffin and starts wailing as he makes contact. Hammering his fists onto the toughened glass, making me wish he would succeed in breaking through and the jagged glass will sever an artery.

However, Massimo has the best that money can buy and I'm guessing the toughened glass is no exception. You could probably drop a heavy weight on it, and it wouldn't budge.

Inside, the mummified remains of his wife stare up at him and I shiver with revulsion and fear. The last time we were here, Massimo promised my own destiny was to swing alongside Wesley over another coffin that has yet to be filled.

Massimo's daughter is the lucky recipient and I pray to God he never finds her because knowing her fate when he does makes me fearful of it ever coming true.

Massimo blames his daughter for his wife's death because she died during childbirth, and he only discovered she was alive at all a few weeks ago. He always thought a friend of mine, Flynn, was his son and instructed Wesley to make the boy's life a living hell for killing his wife.

However, Massimo was tricked, and the real baby was sent away and as it turned out, Wesley himself was Flynn's father.

"Winter!"

Massimo shouts my name and I jump, peering at him

through startled eyes, which I quickly attempt to conceal. Massimo expects me to remain emotionless, an empty doll that he controls and commands, and any sign of humanity is stripped away if it shows itself.

His eyes narrow and I struggle to remain impassive as he beckons me across to the glass coffin.

"Come and pay your respects to Imogen. She wants to see you."

I say nothing and move like an automaton to stand beside the coffin, and he screeches so loud it almost makes me jump.

"Pay your fucking respects, you bitch."

I'm not sure what he wants me to do and as I hover near the coffin, I'm shocked when he grabs my head and slams me face down onto it, almost breaking my nose.

He holds my head firmly and screams, "Look at her! Look at my darling wife. Look at what they did."

I open my eyes and stare into the empty pits of death and decay and the bile rises in my throat as I come face to face with mortality.

"Look at my beautiful bride. They did this to her, those bastards who betrayed me. That bitch who forced her way out of my wife's beautiful defenseless body and took her life along with her. She will pay for that. They will all pay for that, and I will have my delicious revenge."

Once again, he slams my face down hard, and I wonder if my nose is broken. A faint drop of blood spills onto the glass and, if anything, I am fearful of the repercussions of that. Any sign of anything less than perfection is liable to send him into a fearsome rage, and I'm more afraid of that than anything right now.

He starts to wail like a demon burning in hell and I suppose he is. Put there by his own mentality and as he pulls me to my feet, he packs the madness back into its box and smiles, looking around the room as if addressing a crowd. "So, I brought you here to tell you all of my plan, and I think you're going to like it."

He starts to laugh and dance around the room and if I wasn't used to his manic personality by now, this strikes me as the moment he reveals the full extent of his insanity.

"As it turns out, my darlings..." He turns and smiles as if he's a kid on Christmas day and just received his greatest wish.

"Today I am going to win. Today I am going to end this and today I am going to finish what I started all those years ago."

The expression in his eye is different this time. It cuts me deep and chokes me to death. He has changed from the mad murdering bastard into an even more deranged version of himself and he turns to me with all the fury of hell in his eyes and spits, "It turns out that betraying me is a club many seek membership of. Do you remember our old friend Portia Symmons, my darling?" He turns to the coffin and growls, "She has taken me for a fool and sided with my enemies. She thinks she has the right to interfere in our lives, but we both know I am always ten steps ahead of the pack."

The dread curls around my soul edging out the hope that has always lived inside me for an end to this madness as Massimo says with deep anger coating his words, "Today is the day I cleanse my world of all my enemies and you my darling Winter..." he looks at me with triumph, "Will have a front-row seat and watch everyone you ever cared about discover how powerful I really am. Today they lose everything and there is absolutely nothing they can do to prevent it from happening."

CHAPTER 2

ALESSANDRO

My grandfather's jet touches down in Los Angeles, and you could cut the atmosphere with a knife.

The entire trip has been a haze of meetings, plotting the downfall of our greatest enemy and making sure he doesn't see another sunrise.

I've been glad of the distraction because it focuses my mind away from the part of me that's worried things will go wrong. The plan will fail, and I'll lose everyone close to me, hell even my life, but I wouldn't change a thing because the most important thing in my world is to bring Winter back where she belongs.

Just her name alone causes my heart to race and the foundations of my world to shake. It's been so long but seems like yesterday when I held her in my arms. A feeling that's so special, nothing else will ever measure up. Knowing you are holding your destiny in your hands brings with it a powerful responsibility.

You are now accountable for another person's life. Their

safety is your most important mission and to keep the smile on their face is now your life's work.

One night only was all we had, but it counted for everything.

Even when Angelo told us she was married to their father's friend, my love never wavered. It was her worst nightmare coming true and no matter how many people tell me she's happy, I know deep in my heart she's not. She's in a living hell and I'm about to cut the head off the devil holding my woman hostage.

For the past two years, I have lived and breathed Winter Sontauro with one aim in mind. To bring her back to my side, where she belongs.

As we taxi to the stand, my grandfather puffs out a deep sigh, telling me he's not as comfortable with this situation as I believe.

For now, it's just the two of us, our men behind the curtain separating the workers from family. Don Majerio has spent a lifetime building his empire and the tales of his road to damnation make for horrifying listening. Cold, cruel and emotionless in every aspect of life, bar one. His family.

Family is everything to him and it always has been.

Unlike my father.

Rumor has it they fell out and with my grandfather's blessing, my own father gave up his birthright and set up on his own in Boston, leaving his homeland, Sicily, Italy. He turned his back on the family that means so much to my grandfather who set him free on one condition. He must sacrifice his first-born son to take his place, who will inherit the title of Don Majerio on the death of my grandfather. I am that son and my future beckons like a siren dressed in black, her cruel smile promising a life of endless riches, all paid for with the blood and souls of our enemies.

I escaped my fate for two glorious years and lived my

dream as a Hollywood producer. Now the debt is being called in because my own request for help is at the cost of my freedom.

"Have you spoken with your friends?"

My grandfather breaks the silence with a question that surprises me a little, but I nod. "They are in place."

He appears thoughtful before saying with a deep, "Can they be trusted?"

"With my life." I spit out the words as if he dares question their integrity and a wry twist to his lips and a brief shake of his head makes me think I've disappointed him in some way.

"What?" I'm irritable and the word slips out before I check it. The disrespect noted by the gleam in his eye.

It's too late to back down now because that would disappoint him even more and I stare at him with a cold, hard expression of my own, causing a moment's silence to stretch between us like a battle line.

"I trust no one."

His simple statement doesn't surprise me, and I bite back.

"Then I pity you."

To my surprise, he laughs out loud, causing me to stare at him a little harder and then he leans back and raises his glass of whiskey to me in a toast.

"To my successor, who still has a lot to learn."

"That may be, but I'm willing to take risks to get what I want."

I shrug, trying desperately to shake off the black cloud that has settled over my soul. I used to revel in it. Wallow in the pain and enjoy feasting on depression. Not now, not today, because this is the day I get my woman back and that black cloud will be lifted for as long as she remains by my side.

"This woman."

My grandfather surprises me again by referencing the reason I'm here at all.

"Winter." I stare him in the eye and growl my response, causing him to roll his eyes.

"Is she worth it?"

"Yes." A simple word that will never be anything else. Of course, she's worth it. She is everything and I will only become the man my grandfather wants me to be with her by my side.

"You must check emotion, Alessandro."

He shakes his head as if disappointed. "She is your weakness; she may destroy you."

I don't even dignify that with a response and just glare at him with unconcealed rage, causing him to smirk.

"A mafia wife has no place in her husband's heart. She is there as a wife with a job to do."

"Are you saying you never loved Nonna?" I throw it out there because I know how much he adores his wife, and he grins.

"I love my wife; I always have, but I have never given her my heart."

He shrugs. "Possibly because I don't have one. Wouldn't you agree, my savage soldier?"

"Then the rumors are true."

He laughs out loud. "They are fact, not rumor. I love Nonna, but it's a different kind of love. I make my own decisions based on what is good for the family. I treat her like a queen, but she knows her place. She plays no part in my business and never has. My enemies understand that I make no decisions based on her welfare, which is why she has survived this far. That is why I fear for you, Alessandro."

"I don't need your fear."

I shrug and smooth down the creases in my trousers before removing my shades from the breast pocket of my hand tailored Italian suit.

"She makes you weak."

"I disagree."

I know what he's trying to do. He wants me to harden up, be like him, and earn a reputation as an unforgiving unemotional bastard. As I said before, I pity him.

With a deep sigh, he throws back the final dregs of whiskey in his glass and growls, "Then today will either make you the man I know you are deep inside or destroy you with your own weak flaws."

"Which are?" I yawn to prove his words don't get to me and he hisses, "Emotional, trusting and invested."

"Invested?"

He nods. "It's too personal. You've made this business personal, which could be your downfall. One fuck from an eager pussy could crumble years of careful construction. There are other wet pussies, other eager mouths and an endless supply of willing women who would make all your dreams come true. Your weakness is believing in love."

I close my ears to his harsh words because I don't feel like murdering my own grandfather today. I need him too much for that, so I shrug and stand, pulling down the cuffs on my jacket and setting my mood to bastard.

"Thank you for your character assassination, Nonno, but today is about ridding the world of a man who could hold the title as the biggest bastard who ever lived. If you want to help me gift you that title, you must dispose of the only real obstacle in your way."

His keen eyes search my soul as I stand before him and then slowly, as if he hasn't got a nerve in his whole body, he stands and beckons me closer. As he pulls me in for a hug, he whispers, "You are more like me than you want to believe. You may not want this life, but this life wants you and the sooner you realize she's a demanding bitch, the better because she will always be the most important woman in your life and she's a jealous one. Turn your back on her for one second and she will stick a knife in it. Have your fun, Alessandro, but never at the expense of business."

He kisses me on both cheeks and it's at times like this I consider him my grandfather, not the most respected Mafia Don in the world right now.

Now it's time to face the most feared one and with Club Mafia standing alongside my grandfather and the Majerio family, I'm going to get my girl.

CHAPTER 3

WINTER

The car speeds away from Massimo's mansion, and I leave my heart in the nursery. It's not unusual to accompany Massimo on a dinner date and every time we leave it's as if my heart is torn in two because I hate being away from my son, even for a second. Even knowing the bastard beside me is far away from him, I am always fearful that something will happen to Frankie the moment my back is turned.

The fact he is so well cared for makes it bearable somehow. I never meet the people responsible for feeding, bathing and playing with him, but they must be doing a good job because he's a happy baby. Filling out nicely with a healthy glow that settles my heart. I crave every moment I spend with him, always fearful that it's my last, and that sensation is out in force today because of what Massimo told me.

I know better than to ask questions and wait like a timid mouse beside him, knowing he will take great delight in telling me everything. No subject is off limits with him and his favorite one is to describe in great detail how he murders his enemies. Not just enemies, either. There are also the poor unfortunate young men he orders like takeout, who are delivered to his home courtesy of a well-paid servant. Homeless kids fresh off the bus, runaways and guys drunk in dark alleys, all find a home waiting for them chained to his dungeon wall.

He loves to leave the door open as I sit in my cage in my own dark, depressing cell next door, and I hear them scream and beg for their lives as he subjects them to the most depraved ending. I've tried so hard to shut out the screams of a dying man, knowing it won't be quick but a lengthy transition to the afterlife.

There are the times he made me watch, and I tried to block out the violent, despicable images that will live behind my eyes to my dying days. My main fear is that one day a familiar face will replace the strangers I've seen this far. All except one, that is. Corey. The new boyfriend of my friend Emma, who was in the same position the day I was delivered here courtesy of my history teacher. Corey never made it out alive, and I often wonder what Emma went through. They had not long met, but I'm certain she will have forgotten him already. I haven't.

I will always remember him. Praying for his soul, happy he suffers no more.

Knowing there was nothing I could do to save him carved out my own future path. Massimo makes it impossible to fight back. He has stripped my soul of humanity and replaced it with fear. I have no strength left after enduring many months of mental torture and extreme cruelty. I try so hard to focus on the positives to keep me sane and now we are leaving the most important person in my life behind, I must trust Massimo to bring me back to him.

"So, my darling wife, we are in for a treat today."

He sounds eager as he laughs softly. "Now don't be jealous my darling, but I've been meeting another woman in secret."

I say nothing and he nudges me as if we're friends and not prisoner and prison guard. "Portia Symmons was Imogen's boss back in the day. She runs a modeling agency, and my wife was her star model. Imogen was her most beautiful asset and in great demand. Portia is a friend of mine, and we share the same love of fashion and beauty. As soon as I met Imogen, though, she became my world. We were happy and I've never known love like the one we shared."

His voice deepens as he hisses, "Then that bastard baby tore her from my side and my so-called friends covered it up. They betrayed me and we all know how that ended for them."

In a sudden move, he grabs my face and squeezes it hard and hisses, while staring into my eyes. "You will never betray me, will you?"

I try to shake my head, but he does it for me and it's as if he's a dog with his favorite toy. "You love me, don't you, my darling?"

Again, he does it for me and nods my head vigorously, causing my brain to scramble.

Then he holds me by the throat and, to my horror, runs his hand up my leg underneath my skirt, causing my heart to fill with terror as he pushes my panties aside and strokes my clit.

"Who was it?" He snarls as he gazes with fury into my eyes.

"Who took what was mine?"

This is different. He's never been interested in me sexually before and I gasp, "I don't remember."

I've tried so hard to convince him it could have been one of many just to protect Alessandro and the love we had in creating our son and he jabs a cruel finger sharply inside me and hisses, "Do you like that, my darling? Did he do this? Did he take what was mine by rights like the dirty bastard he is?"

I'm so afraid because I've never seen this side of him before and as he pushes in deeper the pain blinds me for a second and then I'm shocked when he slaps me hard around the face and screams, "Whore, you're a fucking whore. I hate you and I hate him. One by one I will string them up and tear out their hearts with my teeth, just you wait." He slaps me hard again, stunning me into disbelief because where has this come from?

The pain is so great I think he must have broken something and as my eyes try to remain focused, he wraps his hands around my throat and squeezes until my breath is torn from my lungs.

"You fucking cheap whore, screwing around behind my back. You were meant to be a virgin. Your father promised you would be a virgin. You are tainted, marked, and imperfect."

My heart fills with fear because once Massimo regards his possessions as imperfect, it sends him into a rage and he replaces them. Is this what's happening? Am I about to lose my life in the back of his car? I almost wish for it but for one thing, my son.

I can't even fight back because I know it would only increase his rage and then almost as soon as it started, it stops, and he releases me and laughs out loud.

"You should see your face, Winter. You know I'm only playing with my favorite doll."

He stares at me with concern and removes a fresh handkerchief from his pocket, dabbing my face and looking annoyed.

"Now I've ruined my amazing makeup. It's such a shame that we will visit my greatest friend and you look anything but perfect."

He pulls me close and starts to groan as if in pain and I feel something hard against my breast. The memory returns from when we visited his old nanny, and he pulled out a tin from his breast pocket. It contained a syringe and a phial of something that caused her to have a massive stroke. Is this his plan? Will he use it on me? Portia, perhaps, or somebody else.

My mind works hard, but there is no chance to act because he pulls back and smiles sheepishly.

"Forgive my games, Winter. It's fun to play, isn't it?"

I smile as if he's my one true love and nod. "You play them so well, my darling."

He fusses around me like a bridesmaid to a bride, attempting to clear up the mess he made, although I'm guessing I bear a mark on my face, judging by how much it throbs. I can't remember the last time I saw my reflection. There are no mirrors in Massimo's world, and I haven't been able to catch a glimpse of my own face since I got here. I wonder what others register when they stare into my eyes. Do they peer behind the smile? Do they witness the pain in my expression? Or do they see what he expects me to portray? A woman in love.

I watch from the inside out and really hope that what happens today won't finally break me.

CHAPTER 4

ALESSANDRO

We travel to the city in convoy. The usual black cars with tinted windows, armed and deadly to anyone who crosses our path. Passing cops look the other way and even the traffic lights change to let us through. The mafia is in town and God help anyone who stands in our way.

As my grandfather's successor, I travel in the car three back from his. My own consigliere is seated beside the driver in front, allowing me some much-needed time on my own.

Taking the opportunity, I pull out my phone and check in with the boss.

"Angelo."

His deep voice offers me comfort, but I detect a note of anxiety as he says quickly, *"Is the plan in motion?"*

"We're on our way. Are you ready?"

"We're all in position."

He falters and I know if I'm emotional, Angelo must be ten times worse because Winter is not just his sister, she's his twin. Part of the same embryo and as close as two people can be and he says gruffly, *"I'm relying on you, Beast."*

He reminds me who I am, and I growl, "I won't let you down."

After a moment's silence, I say urgently, "What about The Savage?"

"In position."

"And The Angel?"

"Running the business operation."

"The Demon?"

"Monitoring the situation and organizing the troops."

"Then it's happening."

So many years of planning have led to this point, and Angelo obviously feels it too as he says in a softer tone, *"Good luck, my friend. I know you will bring her back to me."*

He cuts the call, probably because emotion was getting in the way and neither of us needs that right now.

As I settle back in my seat, I think about my friends all playing their parts in bringing Winter home. Ever since our days at Rockwell Academy we have been planning this. Initially, the plan was to escape our hated fathers and carve out our own path in life. Then Winter was stolen, and it became much more.

Angelo was the first to kill his father and take control of the Sontauro family. Then Flynn married Louisa and earned the support of her father and godfather, the Columbian drugs baron Pedro Carlos.

Then Ivan kidnapped Charlotte, Massimo's stolen daughter, supplying us with the secret weapon to bring him down.

Angelo is on his way to Massimo's home. Flynn is covering his businesses and every home and asset Massimo owns is about to be taken from him with the help of several families who have pledged their allegiance to us.

Ivan and Charlotte have a special job to do and, along with my grandfather, I'm the one responsible for taking the man himself out.

I am trying so hard not to think of Winter. So many times I have imagined seeing her again. Has she changed? Will she still be the woman I've held tenderly in my mind? I remember her soft body against mine and the way her eyes lit up when she saw me. The taste of her and the pleasure of tearing through her virginity and discovering a place I was immediately at home. I fell in love with Winter long before I claimed her greatest gift. That just reinforced the fact we were meant to be together. How will I react when she walks into Scarpetta? I can't let emotion control me today. My grandfather was right about that because it could blow this whole plan apart.

As my grandfather's car cuts free from ours and is flanked by one before and after it, my own is escorted to Scarpetta to take our places for the show.

We have worked tirelessly going over the plans a hundred times over, allowing for any eventuality and yet I can't shake the anxiety from clouding my mind. It *must* work, failure is not an option and as we stop outside the restaurant, Tommaso, my consigliere, wrenches open the door and says coolly, "Sir."

I merely nod and step outside into the sunshine, looking a strange sight dressed all in black, my dark hair scraped back into a ponytail and the matching silk shirt and tie in place, looking so wrong against the heat of the day.

My men keep watch as I make my way inside and I am met by the maitre d who looks as if he would prefer to have called in sick rather than face this horror show.

"Mr. Majerio. We are honored."

He almost bows as I glare at him and snap. "Is my table as instructed?"

He nods and grabs a menu, scurrying before me, saying, "Of course, please follow me."

As I walk through the restaurant, a hush falls on the room courtesy of the curiosity thrown my way by the other diners. As I take my seat behind a pillar with a view to the last remaining table, I note the atmosphere and my heart sinks. Fucking mafia. Each and every one. No wonder the maitre d looks as if he's about to win a trip to the emergency room.

The terror lingers in the air as every table is filled with men. All in black suits making it appear as if we're extras for the latest Godfather movie.

I don't miss the curious stares and guarded expressions of the men as they look my way. They know who I am—what I am, and I wonder what is running through their minds right now. Hell, I'm trying not to think of what's running through my own mind and so I settle back and snap, "Whiskey, make it a double."

I can almost sense my grandfather's disapproval from here and he's not even made it into the room yet. Fuck a clear head, anyway. I work better with a little Dutch courage inside me.

The clock on the wall reveals we have twenty minutes until showtime and so I settle back and prime myself for a war—a mafia war and this time the stakes are high.

CHAPTER 5

WINTER

Massimo is excited. The way he taps his foot and exhales sharply sets me on edge. He is in his element right now. Plotting and scheming another man's downfall and I'm not shocked when he starts cackling like the evillest wizard.

"This is going to be so much fun."

He starts rocking back and forth and giggles like a small child.

"I love games, don't you, Winter? You see, I am a master at chess and your friends are going to find out why."

"My friends?"

I'm surprised because I understood we were meeting his friend, Portia Symmons.

His head snaps my way, making me regret speaking at all. I spoke outside of a direct question, and he hates that. His eyes narrow and I resign myself to what happens next as he clicks his tongue and says harshly, "Naughty girl, speaking without permission."

He slams his hand against my mouth and pushes me back against the seat, grabbing my earlobe and twisting it cruelly, causing the tears to well up in my eyes as he inflicts pain on me.

Almost immediately, he releases me and sneers, "Next time I won't be so kind. Now, what do you say?"

"I'm sorry, my darling, please forgive me."

He looks at me for a moment as if he's thinking carefully, and then he unbuckles my seatbelt and says roughly, "On your knees before me."

Shaking, I do as he asks and as he lays his hand on the top of my head, he whispers, "I forgive you, my child."

He offers me the back of his hand and I press my lips to it and whisper, "Thank you, my darling."

He pulls his hand away and tilts my face to his and the triumphant gleam in his eyes makes the nausea rise inside me.

"I will tell you a secret, my darling, because you have pleased me."

I stare up at him and he grins. "I had word that the restaurant was booked out. There were no spare tables at all, and any previous bookings were canceled and replaced by new ones."

I continue to stare, and he twists his lips into a grin.

"They believe I'm a fool. Setting a trap they hoped I would walk right into."

He throws his head back and laughs and says with a dark tone to his voice, "My men are under instructions to wipe out the enemy and replace them. When Portia turns up with her mysterious date, I will have them cornered."

He pats his breast pocket and winks. "You remember Iris Young, my former nanny, don't you, darling?"

I nod, still kneeling before him, trying desperately to stay still despite the rocking movements of the car.

"Well…" he laughs out loud. "Portia is about to join her. Strokes are so damaging, aren't they, my darling? I have a bed set up beside my beloved nanny and they can keep each other company. My aim is to liberate them to my home and allow them to spin beside Wesley in the future, but for now they will live out their days waiting for my next move, not knowing what or when that will be."

Once again, he pats the top of my head and grins. "So, Portia and her friend become my latest casualties. I'm guessing the person with her intends on challenging my authority, so they must be quite powerful. I'm really hoping it's one of your friends, Winter. Wouldn't that be delightful watching me tear him apart in my dungeon? I'll even allow you to assist me. So much fun is on the horizon, wouldn't you agree?"

I feel sick inside, hoping to God he's wrong, but maintain a blank expression and smile.

"I can't wait, my darling."

He sighs and for a moment looks like a boy searching for his mother as he says in a small voice, "I need a hug."

He takes my hand and pulls me onto his knee and whispers, "Hug me, my darling. Show me how much you love me."

It takes all my strength to wrap my arms around his neck and as he rocks me like a baby, he makes small pitiful noises, like an animal in pain. Then he looks up and before I register what's happening, his lips fasten against mine and he forces his tongue down my throat as he grips my head hard, forcing me to accept the most disgusting kiss of my life as his saliva fills my mouth making me gag.

Without warning, he slaps me away and shrieks, "You fucking whore! What are you doing?"

I'm in shock as he strikes me around the face again and again before slamming my head against the window.

I can't fight the fear that engulfs me and just when I think he's about to end my life, the car stops suddenly and he says pleasantly, "Gather yourself together, my darling. I hope you're hungry. I know I am."

To anyone watching, he is the image of a successful businessman and I look like a cheap whore who serviced him on the way over. My clothes are creased and my hair is all over the place. I'm guessing the throbbing in my face is the result of a damaging bruise and my neck is sore where he nearly squeezed the life out of me. I'm almost positive my lipstick is smeared across my face and the tears in my eyes are causing my make-up to streak. I am far from the perfect doll right now and I'm fearful about what that means for me. I am imperfect, soiled and broken. I am fast approaching my use by date and the only possible outcome will be a cruel and painful transition to hell.

We stop suddenly and as the door opens, Massimo steps out and offers me his hand.

As I step into the light, I see the unguarded look of horror on Massimo's soldier's face before it is replaced by indifference. I walk beside my abuser as if I'm walking to the gallows because I know how this works. Massimo is out to cause havoc and pain, and it appears the person first in line for that is me.

CHAPTER 6

ALESSANDRO

My gun is heavy against my heart, reminding me what's at stake. As I observe the two new diners heading into the restaurant, it's safe in the knowledge I'm concealed from view. I pay attention to the woman eagerly, searching her expression, wondering if she knows how serious this is.

I'm guessing she must be in her sixties, but you would never guess. Apparently, surgery has been kind to her because every inch of skin appears to have been nipped and tucked into place, defying nature's best intentions.

Portia Symmons is a fine-looking woman, and the fact my grandfather's hand is placed on the small of her back signifies an ownership and an intimacy that sickens me.

I am trying to remember the last time he escorted my grandmother anywhere. I'm guessing his nights are spent with different company and Nonna is probably happy to be off the hook.

It's well known my grandfather likes the women. He's an Italian Stallion of the greediest kind.

The way Portia smiles up at him and flutters her eyelashes

tells me she adores him, and I fight back a grin because the old man is a player and I suppose he always will be.

I'm pretty certain the sparkling diamond around her neck would be a gift from him, and I'm guessing the fake tits are also a well-earned reward.

I watch with interest as they take their seats facing the door so they can observe the man of the hour and his soon to be widow walk on stage.

The maitre d fusses over my grandfather and Portia as if they are visiting royalty and as soon as he heads off to bring their drinks, I endure them fawning over each other like teenagers on a date after the game.

All the time my mind is wired when I think about what happens next. Finally, I will be in the same room, breathing the same oxygen as the woman I love, and I'm not sure how I'll deal with that.

Twenty minutes pass and I can tell my grandfather is getting angrier by the second. He is the most impatient man I know and even the hand job Portia gave him under the table hasn't mellowed his mood.

Then the door opens, and I swear my heart almost gives out on me when Massimo Delauren and Winter walk into the packed room.

Nothing prepares me for seeing her in the flesh for the first time in two years. It's as if the years melt away and I'm seeing her walking from Principal Stoner's office. I don't do feelings and certainly never emotion, but watching her slight body move through the restaurant, it's a direct hit straight to my heart.

I can't tear my eyes from her.

Nobody else matters as I stare hungrily at a woman that has occupied my dreams for the past two years.

I love her.

It happened so fast and hard it took me a while to understand what that means. I will do anything for her, and it takes every ounce of self-control I possess not to jump up and go to her, tearing her hand from the man who deserves to die in the most horrific way.

I'm not the only one who can't tear their eyes from the scene and as Massimo holds her hand and leads her through the tables like the most precious bone china, I barely manage to conceal my rage when I see the purple bruise that covers half of her face. The marks on her neck almost make me lose my mind, but it's the fear in her once sparkling eyes that sends me over the edge.

Despite everything, though, my soul weeps bitter tears for the woman I love, for the life she has endured since she left my side and for the pain she must suffer daily because of *him*.

I can't even look at him because one second of my attention away from Winter is a second wasted and I drink in every drop of her features and feast on a dish I have craved for so long it hurts.

The fact they can't see me provides me with a golden opportunity and I stare so hard she must surely feel it from where she's standing.

She looks so frail, so battered, and so weary. Not the effortless, cold beauty my friends described. There is no love in the gaze that lingers on her face when she turns to her husband. She is a prisoner of circumstance and I intend on blasting the door wide open and so I bite back my anger and gain strength from her weakness. I feed off it to use against the man she stands beside, and I make a vow that he dies today in the most painful way I can make happen.

Winter

I'm not sure how I can even walk. My legs are shaking so much. The restaurant is packed, and I don't miss the nervous glances thrown my way as we pass through the tables. They must be horrified by my appearance because it looks as if I've been in a car wreck. I'm certain of that, and I wonder why Massimo flipped the way he did. There must be a reason for it, there always is, and yet why would he want these people to see me this way?

We take our seats and I stare at a beautiful, graceful woman who looks at me with a shocked smile. The gentleman beside her has a familiar appearance that I can't place, and he is staring at me with a curious fascination that's a little unnerving.

I don't miss the frostiness between him and Massimo, who says tightly, "Don Majerio. I wasn't aware you knew Portia."

The name jumps out and hits me far harder than Massimo did.

Majerio.

Alessandro Majerio, the beast I fell in love with. Frankie's father and the man I left my heart to keep forever.

As I stare at the gentleman who bears the same name, it only reinforces the similarity. Is this his father, grandfather, an uncle perhaps? The similarities are breath-taking and my heart flutters and then starts galloping as his husky drawl enters the conversation.

"Don Delauren. It's been many years."

"You never answered my question." Massimo snaps, and the hint of amusement in Don Majerio's face makes me curious.

He turns to Portia and rests his arm along the back of her chair and says lazily, "Portia is a good friend of mine, too."

"Friends with benefits, I'm guessing." Massimo fires back and I can tell he's nervous just from the tapping of his foot under the table.

Massimo clicks his fingers and the waiter heads over as if

he's running the 100m and Massimo says sulkily, "A bottle of your finest vintage champagne. It appears we have a celebration on our hands."

"We do?"

Don Majerio arches his brow and Massimo growls, "Yes, today we celebrate friendship and new beginnings."

I turn my attention to Portia, who is looking mighty uncomfortable, and she grabs her glass of water and almost drains it entirely, which Massimo seizes on immediately.

"You appear nervous, Portia. Is there a reason for that?"

His cool tone obviously registers with her, and she says shakily, "No, it's just, well, I wasn't aware the two of you were acquainted."

"I don't believe you."

Her eyes widen as Massimo snarls, "In fact, I'm making an educated guess that you set this whole thing up, Portia."

She looks startled and moves back a little as if to distance herself, causing her guest to lean forward and say with an undercurrent of danger, "Back off Massimo. Portia has nothing to do with this."

Massimo merely laughs out loud and waves around him. "She may not, but it's obvious you do."

Shaking his head, he gestures at the silent tables. "Did you really believe I would be foolish enough to walk into your trap, Don Majerio?"

He says nothing and Massimo starts rocking in his seat, laughing like a clown.

"You will never beat me. Nobody will ever beat me because I am invincible."

He stops and grabs my hair and twists it cruelly and snarls, "Look at my wife. I control every part of her. She depends on me and can't bear to be without me. Isn't that right, my darling?"

He nods my head for me and the distaste in Don Majerio's

eyes makes my heart sink. He is no match for Massimo. He must know he is about to face death and lose the fight because one by one, every man in the restaurant stands and takes out their guns.

Massimo laughs like a maniac and, still holding my hair, snarls, "You've had a good run, Don Majerio but the race is over."

He glares at Portia and snarls, "I have a particular fate waiting for you, my friend. Tell her, Winter, tell her how merciless I am when faced with betrayal."

The tears course down my face as I fight the pain and just gasp, "He's merciless."

Massimo laughs like a hyena and then something happens that takes us all by surprise as the door opens and two new diners enter the room. Portia and Don Majerio glance past us, and a small smile breaks out across the Don's face, and he smirks as he says to Massimo, "It appears we have a visitor."

Dropping me like a hot poker, Massimo turns, and I see his expression change as he stares at the two people who are heading toward us. My own mouth drops as a familiar face reveals itself and I whisper, "Ivan."

The tears fall unchecked because who cares about appearances now when I see the Savage who protected me so well at Rockwell academy heading into the restaurant, holding the hand of the woman from the painting. Imogen. Massimo's wife.

The chair falls back as he stands and stumbles toward her with a disbelieving cry.

"Imogen, my darling."

The whole restaurant stills as he cries, "Where have you been? I waited for you."

He falters a little and shakes his head as if he's seeing a ghost, and I suppose in his mad mind, he is.

"Darling, you must have been so afraid. Were you lost? Did

you ache for me as I have ached for you? We have so much to catch up on. Tell me the names of the people responsible for keeping me from you, and I will ensure their long and painful death. You can help me; we will be a team again. Where's the baby?"

He looks around wildly and then screams, "WHERE'S THE BABY? WHO TOOK OUR BABY?"

He howls like an animal in pain, and I don't believe one person here expected to see this sight today. The real Massimo Delauren in all his chaotic glory. The mask has slipped and shattered to the ground as he struggles to separate the past from the present.

The expression on the girl's face is terror personified as she holds on tightly to Ivan's hand, who is staring at Massimo with all the fury of Satan himself. As Massimo lurches forward, Ivan steps in front of her and snarls, "Back off Massimo."

Massimo stops as if stunned and his voice breaks a little. "Who are you? Why are you holding my wife's hand?"

He turns to his soldiers and shrieks, "Kill him!"

He looks wildly around and stares in disbelief as every last soldier lowers their guns and he can be in no doubt of their intentions as they stare at him with hate and disgust.

"What are you waiting for? Kill the bastard! Kill them all. I order you!"

The silence is palpable as Massimo stares in confusion around him and then his eyes flick back to the woman he believes is his dead wife. The expression on his face is one of pain, confusion, and hope. He has so much love and need in his eyes as he stares at the woman he loved before she died so cruelly, and witnessing the uncertainty in his daughter's expression makes my heart break for her. Just picturing her fate lying beside her mother in perpetuity fills my soul with pain and then, from out of nowhere, a voice from the past whispers in my ear and I hear his words as clear as the day I heard them.

"Learn how to survive and always look for their weakness because there always is one. Then use that to your advantage to get what you want. The element of surprise is a powerful weapon, and I'm guessing you can learn to wield it where it will do the most damage."

Now is that time. My opportune moment because Massimo can't tear his eyes away from the woman I must save. I steal a furtive glance around me and it's as if the packed restaurant is frozen in time as they witness a scene play out that is so unbelievable it doesn't seem real.

I note that Massimo's men's guns are lowered as they view something they would never have believed, and Portia is staring in disbelief at the woman who is the spitting image of her mother. Don Majerio appears as stunned as the rest of us and nobody gives me a second glance as I reach into Massimo's jacket that he hung on the back of his chair.

I hold my breath as the seconds tick down to the end of life as I know it and my heart races as my fingers close around the metal box that contains the deadliest injection.

My hands shake as I attempt to remove it under the cover of the table, and when I feel the plastic syringe in my hand, I relish the sense of power at my disposal.

Massimo continues to stare at his daughter in disbelief as she cowers behind her husband. Ivan, meanwhile, is preparing to tear Massimo limb from limb if he has to.

Carefully, I edge slowly toward him and as I reach his side, he doesn't even see me and without any hesitation, I plunge the needle deep into the side of his neck.

As I release the steady stream of poison into his bloodstream, his scream tears the city apart and all around us the spectators stand frozen in shock as he stumbles and reaches out, grabbing me roughly by the shoulders.

"What have you done? You stupid bitch, you'll pay dearly for this!"

His piercing scream bounces off the walls and before anyone can react to what's happening, he falls toward me. I have no time to step aside and it's as if the whole scene is in slow motion as Massimo's giant frame crashes against me, forcing me back and as we fall to the ground as one, a glancing blow on the back of my head fills my final breath with pure agony.

CHAPTER 7

ALESSANDRO

I almost couldn't concentrate on the job I was given. As soon as Winter walked into the room, my mind left me. It was the most difficult thing in my life not to pounce. To tear her husband apart in front of the packed restaurant for daring to breathe the same air as her. The fact he obviously laid his hands on her made my blood fizz like a volcano on the edge of eruption.

My instructions were clear. Take the bastard out with one bullet from my gun at the perfect moment as soon as Ivan and Charlotte walked into the room. That was my cue, the distraction I needed and as I raised my gun and trained it on the target, even I wasn't prepared for what happened next.

Massimo's men played their part perfectly. I've got to hand it to my grandfather, he knows his stuff and buying every single last fucking one out was a stroke of pure genius. Massimo's men have been living under a storm cloud for years now and being assured of their protection was enough to get them to switch sides. Massimo thought he had won and had outsmarted the fox but every single fucking body in Scarpetta was intent on ending his life today.

Before I could finish the job, Winter made her move, and the gun shook in my grip when she moved to his side. It happened so quickly I had no time to think and when she stabbed him in the neck, it took me a moment to understand what was happening. When he fell, it was in slow motion, in my head, anyway, and before he even hit the deck, I was on my feet and running.

I am the first to reach them and it takes minimum effort to tear his body from hers and with an angry roar, I swing my arm back and relish the sound of bone shattering as I knock the bastard clean across the room, shouting, "Ivan, deal with this bastard."

Massimo's agonized screams are the best sound in the world as his body reacts to whatever Winter did to him, coupled with the pain from my own rage.

My trusted friend needs no further instruction and I sense Massimo's body being dragged away and I hope it's to fucking hell.

The chaos you would expect to follow an incident like this never happens. Instead, the men watch as if they are frozen to the spot. My attention is now focused on only one thing and as I drop to my knees, the emotion inside me threatens to tear me apart. I briefly hear my grandfather's firm, authoritative voice say roughly, "Call the doctor."

It all pales into white noise around me as I drop beside my woman and as I reach down and pull her into my arms, the emotion almost overwhelms me.

She looks so beaten, so tragic and nothing like the woman who radiated happiness the last time we met. Her body is frail and so thin it tears my heart apart and squeezes it in a vise like grip, causing me unimaginable pain.

Her skin is white, and her eyes closed against the terror that lives inside them and as I lower my face to hers, I experience a huge wave of relief when I detect shallow breaths telling me she still lives for now.

The open wound on the back of her head is of concern and grabbing the napkin from the table, I hold it against the back of her skull, applying pressure to stem the flow.

I almost can't speak. The emotions are swirling inside me like an advancing enemy, either promising me a slow painful death or preparing me for the fight of my life.

"Winter." My voice shakes a little as I try to reach her, and then I raise it a little, more out of fear than anything else.

"Winter baby, it's Alessandro. You're safe now. Open your eyes."

She resembles the Sleeping Beauty in my arms and like the prince who stumbled upon her own lifeless body, I press my lips to hers in the foolish hope that fairy tales are an actual thing, and this is all it will take to bring her back to me.

I have pictured this moment a trillion times since she was taken, but nothing prepared me for the pain I'm experiencing knowing she is hurt.

"Alessandro." My grandfather's husky voice reaches through the darkness and his hand on my shoulder reminds me I'm not alone.

"The doctor is on his way."

Portia drops down beside me and says firmly, "We must apply pressure to the wound."

She hands me fresh napkins and as I hold my angel in my arms, I am grateful for their support.

I don't even register that the restaurant has emptied, and it's just the four of us crowding around Winter. The time stretches interminably as we wait for professional help.

Charlotte hands me another napkin and whispers, "She is so brave."

I am surrounded by well-meant actions, but I want them to

go. I want to be alone with my beautiful woman and it will take a strong man to tear her from my arms.

Charlotte kneels on the other side of me and takes her hand, causing me to snarl, "What are you doing?"

Her firm response reminds me why she is a match made in heaven for my irascible friend as she ignores the undercurrent of anger in my voice and says firmly, "Checking for a pulse. We need to assess the situation and just holding her and hoping she's ok is not going to work I'm afraid."

She looks at Portia and says briskly, "We need to clear some space. Move some of these tables and bring more napkins to stem the blood flow."

She looks at my grandfather and says firmly, "Go and find the emergency first aid kit in this place. They must have one. It's the law, you know."

To my surprise, my grandfather doesn't even question her command and then she places her hand on my arm and says with a hint of steel in her voice, "Is she breathing, Alessandro?"

"Yes." My voice shakes and I hate the emotion that is filling my heart.

"Good, we need to check her vital signs."

I can't even speak and as Charlotte searches for a pulse and checks her breathing, I allow her to fuss around Winter like the best emergency room nurse as I openly stare at the woman I love and whisper, "Winter baby, please open your eyes, it's Alessandro. Angelo is on his way. You're safe now."

At the mention of Angelo, I hope to God Ivan is briefing him now and as the door opens to the restaurant, I barely register the person entering until my grandfather says, "Alessandro, the doctor is here. Stand aside."

I can't even move and just the thought of moving away from Winter is like a knife to my heart but then Charlotte rests her hand on my arm and says softly, "The best way to help her now is to let the professionals work their magic."

I know she's right and as I tear myself away, it's like a physical punch to the gut as the doctor does what he was trained to do.

It doesn't take long before the restaurant is filled with activity as the paramedics arrive and crowd around Winter. Charlotte stands beside me and places a comforting hand on my shoulder, reminding me I'm not alone in this, even though it definitely feels that way.

I try so hard to drag my mind back to business and my hand shakes a little as I type out a text to the Boss.

> **The target is down, but Winter was injured. Meet us at the emergency room. She took a blow to the head when she fell. The paramedics are here now. I'll go with her.**

I watch as the team lifts her onto a stretcher and the doctor says loudly, "We need to get her to the hospital. Vital signs are good, but she's unresponsive."

My grandfather nods and catches my eye and I see the pain in his as he sighs. "Keep me informed."

I nod and as I follow the medics out, I pray to God to bring Winter back to me because I would sell my soul to the devil a million times over just to see her smile again.

CHAPTER 8

ALESSANDRO

The ride in the ambulance is short and sweet yet seems to last a lifetime. All the way to the hospital, the medics do their stuff, leaving me sitting watching, feeling more helpless than I have ever felt in my life.

As soon as we reach the hospital, she is whisked away and I am left to wait in the hope they can bring her back to me.

Almost as soon as she disappears through the doors, the emergency room fills up with more black suits than a wake as Angelo storms the building with his usual entourage. The fear on the nurses faces is almost laughable as Angelo's men do what they are trained to do and cover every exit and glare with menace at anyone who dares to look at them. As Angelo rushes to my side, the pain and fear on his face will live with me to my dying day.

"Where is she?"

I jerk my thumb toward the door and say huskily, "She fell and hit her head on the corner of the table. She has a head wound and is unconscious."

"But she's alive."

"She's alive."

Angelo nods but I can tell he's shit scared, and it strikes me this is what it's like to be helpless and I don't like it at all.

The nurse approaches us tentatively and says with a slight catch to her voice, "Um, we have a private room you can wait in. Perhaps you would all be more comfortable in there."

She glances at the soldiers who just stare around them with no emotion and Angelo nods. "Thank you."

He turns to his consigliere, Roberto and says firmly, "Secure the entrance, and instruct the rest to wait in the car."

The nurse looks relieved as Roberto nods and one by one, the men leave.

We follow the nurse to the room she decided was the best way to deal with the situation and as she leaves us to it, Angelo prowls around like a panther.

"What happened?"

As I fill him in, I sense his anger growing because I hold nothing back.

"He hit her?' His voice is laced with retribution, and I nod. "She was a mess, Boss. Her face and neck were bruised, and it looked as if he'd roughed her up on the journey over."

My voice breaks as I say angrily, "I swear to God it was the hardest thing I have ever had to do to stick with the plan because all I wanted was to tear the fucking bastard apart with my bare hands."

Angelo nods. "Where is he?"

"Ivan dragged him off somewhere."

"Is he still alive?"

"I'm not sure."

Angelo growls, "I fucking hope he is, because I want to make his death a long and painful one."

A hesitant knock on the door grabs our attention and as it opens, Charlotte's anxious face peers into the room.

"I'm sorry, I hope you don't mind, but Ivan asked his men to bring me here."

Angelo nods. "Of course, it's fine. Grab a seat."

"Have you heard anything?"

I don't miss the frightened expression in her eyes and that the dress she is wearing is stained with Winter's blood and for the first time, I register it on my own hands. Angelo also notices it and the fury in his expression makes me hope that Massimo still breathes because, like my friend, I want to be the one to take his last one.

"She'll be ok." Charlotte's voice quivers and I'm sure she's saying that more as a wish than anything else.

"She has to be." Angelo growls and as Charlotte drops down into the seat beside me, her voice is full of concern as she touches my arm and whispers, "Are you ok?"

I will *never* be ok all the time Winter is at risk and I shake my head. "No."

She sighs and leans back, saying sadly, "I hope he's dead."

Suddenly, we remember just who is sitting here and we stare at her as her voice shakes. "It was obvious he was deranged. Thank God Winter acted so fast. I was so afraid."

Angelo lowers his voice. "We would never have put you in danger without protection. I'm just sorry you had to meet him at all."

"I'm not." She exhales sharply and forces a brighter tone to her voice. "At least I looked him in the eye and saw the madness for myself. The only thing that scares the living daylights out of me is that I've inherited some of it."

Just looking at the sweet, pretty blonde who looks as if she was spun from cotton candy makes my lips twitch for a second and Angelo's own expression softens as he quips, "I think you're right."

"Excuse me." She looks up in alarm and he says with a smile, "Any woman who marries a savage must be mentally disturbed. We'll get you professional help. God knows you'll need it."

She shakes her head and points her finger at him, making

me grin. "You leave my husband out of this. He's one of the good ones."

Angelo bites back a grin as Charlotte jumps up. "I'll go and fetch us some coffee. Obviously, I would prefer tea, but I guess that's probably not an option."

She makes to leave, and Angelo says firmly, "Sit down."

She spins around and he sighs. "Ivan was right to send you here. You need protection and setting you free in this hospital is not an option. I'll organize the coffee, and I *will* fetch you a tea, just in case you think we are all savages."

She drops back into her seat with a shocked expression on her face as Angelo opens the door and places our order with one of the soldiers outside.

As he slams it shut behind him, he raises his eyes. "Consider it done."

"I'll never get used to this."

Charlotte shakes her head and I growl, "You're one of us now. We look after our own."

She smiles but I see the concern in her eyes as she whispers, "She'll be ok."

"What are you, a doctor now?" I grin to remove the bite from my words, and she shrugs. "I've studied first aid and am quite the fan of hospital drama. She'll pull through, just you see."

We all fall silent as we pray for the same thing. To get Winter back and lose her so quickly just isn't a fucking option. Of course she'll make it. She has to.

* * *

It must be two hours later the doctor pays us a visit and his blank expression gives nothing away as he says wearily, "Is one of you her husband?"

Angelo steps forward. "I'm her brother."

The doctor nods. "She's stable but unresponsive. She suffered a head trauma, but there is nothing on the scan telling us we need to operate. To be safe, we have placed her in an induced coma to give her brain time to function properly. We should know more in a few days."

"Will she be ok?"

Angelo asks the question we all need the answer to and, as always, the doctor gives nothing away.

"There is no obvious damage. As I said, we will monitor her."

"I want to see her?"

Angelo's tone doesn't give the doctor many options and with a sigh, he nods. "Of course, only you, though."

I jump up. "Not happening. We all go."

I fix the doctor with my most fearsome expression and he swallows hard. "Maybe in this case we'll bend the rules a little."

He sighs. "Follow me."

We walk behind him, and I swear my heart is thumping because I'm not sure if I can hold my shit together. Angelo looks destroyed and Charlotte anxious and as we head toward the ICU, I die a thousand times inside.

The doctor stops outside a room and a huge window gives us a view inside and we see the frail body of the woman we have ached to bring back to us wired up to frightening machines, looking like an angel hovering between heaven and earth.

Angelo glances at me and for a moment we share the same emotion. I understand exactly what he is going through right now, and I can tell he thinks the same. The doctor cuts through the emotion and says wearily, "You must gown up and scrub up if you want to go inside. One at a time though, the room is too small for a party."

He pales as two dark stares fix on him and he stutters, "Well, anyway, I should be um, heading back. Leave your details at reception and we'll keep you informed of any changes."

He scurries off, and Charlotte shakes her head as she watches him go. "You could have thanked him. That was awfully rude, you know. The poor man, I didn't know where to look. I was so embarrassed."

She sighs and says quickly, "Well, what are you waiting for, scrub up boys, Winter's waiting."

CHAPTER 9

ALESSANDRO

Almost as soon as Angelo heads inside the room, Ivan appears looking like the savage he is.

His rough expression falls on his wife, who runs into his open arms and as his strong tattooed ones fold around her, I envy him. He has secured her future with him. Nothing will ever tear them apart and they have one another. My gaze flicks inside the room and my heart twists when I see Angelo smooth the hair away from his sister's eyes as he raises her hand to his lips. It's such a gentle act of brotherly love that hits me hard. If I am in hell, he is right beside me because we are facing the unknown and I don't think either of us can deal with that.

Ivan steps closer and growls, "Fucking bastard."

His arm is slung around Charlotte's shoulders and for a second we just stare at the scene inside the room.

"Where is he?" I growl and Ivan snaps, "Heading on vacation to Italy."

Charlotte gasps, "Is he alive?"

Ivan laughs darkly. "Some might say he's hovering between life and death."

"What's that supposed to mean?" I growl and Ivan places a

comforting arm on my back and says softly, "It means he's no longer a threat, my friend. We'll keep him alive until the boss says otherwise."

Charlotte's voice shakes. "Will I have to see him again?"

"No." Ivan's response is firm, and she exhales sharply. "Good. Once was enough."

I say under my breath, "And Massimo's men?"

"You mean *my* men."

My heart sags with relief. "So, the plan worked."

Ivan nods. "You are now looking at Don Volkov. I have my army, now I just need a fortress."

He turns to Charlotte. "It's time to go house hunting, malyshka."

"What do you mean?" Her eyes are wide as he whispers, "Your father's business is now mine. What's left of it, anyway."

"Since when?"

"Since Alessandro's grandfather made the deal. We rid the world of the bastard and they switch their loyalty to me. I am currently without my own Bratva, so it makes perfect sense to remain here and take everything Massimo owns. The fact we torched all his assets is a minor problem, but we'll find new premises, a new home, and make it work."

He says in a low voice, "Flynn reported back that the operation was a success. Pedro Carlos and his men moved in and wiped out his South American operation, and the Romanos dealt with any Florida business. The Morettis took Chicago and Flynn took care of the mid-west and Angelo dealt with the Californian business."

"So, there's nothing left."

I think about the scale of the operation that involved many alliances with rival families and I can't believe we did it. However, none of it means shit all the time the woman responsible for the attack hovers between life and death.

Angelo heads outside and nods. "Your turn."

I don't even wait to hear what he says because I'm taking his place before the door even closes.

The room is silent save for the machines wired up to the woman I love, keeping her alive until she wakes up and comes back to me.

As I approach the bed, I've never experienced such agony because there is absolutely nothing I can do to help her.

She looks so small, so pale, and so lifeless. The machine breathes for her and the purple bruises covering her face and neck are the only color on her skin.

As I take the seat Angelo just vacated, I reach for her hand, and it's so small and soft in mine. My chest tightens as I struggle to breathe because there is so much I want to say to the woman I love and grieved for over the past two years.

"Winter baby, it's Alessandro."

If I thought that would change anything, I'm a fool because there is no reaction at all. I lean closer and press my lips to hers and it's like a homecoming. How I've ached to feel those lips on mine and imagined her in my arms. Not like this though, never like this and it's the purest agony knowing there is nothing I can do to help her.

As I hold her hand, I hope she can hear me when I whisper, "I waited for you, baby. There has never been anyone but you. Always you. The night we shared is my happiest and sweetest memory. When you were taken, I died a little that day. Since then, I've thought of nothing else but bringing you back to me. I love you, Winter Sontauro, and I've never stopped. If anything, the love grew into the beast inside me. Stronger, angrier, and more passionate. It's only ever been you and always will be, so come back to me, Winter, and let me prove it for the rest of our lives."

My reply is the noise from the machine, which is the only indication she is alive at all. She sleeps like Snow White in her glass coffin. Pale white skin, ruby red lips and black shiny hair.

She is my princess and always will be and there is nothing on earth that will tear me away from her side.

The door opens and Angelo says gruffly, "I need a moment."

I experience a physical pain inside as I'm forced to drop her hand and as I swap places with her brother, I hate every step I take away from her.

Charlotte peers at me with concern. "Alessandro, you should grab some sleep."

Ivan rolls his eyes. "You think he can sleep?"

He turns to her and cups her face in his rough hands and whispers, "Do you think I would sleep if you were in that bed? Do you possibly imagine I would take one step from your side? You are stating an impossible fact because my friend will only walk out of here with his woman beside him."

Charlotte's eyes glitter with tears as she nods, her husband's emotion striking where it was intended. Her heart. Ivan flicks a glance toward the glass window and the pain in his expression reminds me we all loved Winter in our way.

"Are you ok man?" I rest my hand on his back and he nods.

"I'll be ok when Winter wakes up. We all will."

Angelo heads outside and says with a sigh. "I'll find the doctor. Ivan…" he turns to our savage friend and says firmly, "Take Charlotte back to the house. Roberto will arrange it. You have an empire to build and can't hang around."

"But Winter."

"We will inform you if anything changes. Flynn is setting my phone on fire, and I wouldn't put it past him to show up. Malik is dealing with all the shit on his own right now, so put your house in order. We've come too far to let this fail now."

Ivan is conflicted and as his eye catches mine, I jerk my head toward Charlotte. It appears the adrenalin is wearing off and the shock is beginning to hit her.

He stares at his wife and his expression softens. He nods. "I want to know the minute she wakes up. We all do."

He takes his wife's hand and smiles softly. "Let's get you home."

Her tired eyes flicker between us, and she hesitates for a moment and then says sadly, "I never met Winter until today, but I have heard a lot about her. I understand how special she is to you all and watching her bravery in the middle of a potential gunfight makes me admire her more than anyone I've ever met. She's strong, and women that fight back continue to fight. It may not look like it now, but inside, Winter is fighting to come back to you, and you know what, she will make it. You wait and see."

We stare at the fragile beauty who has more strength than anybody would imagine, and her pure emotion wraps us all in comfort. It's almost too much, so I say with amusement, "What are you, a fortune teller now as well as a doctor?"

My friends smirk as she grins. "You better believe it. It's called manifestation and I'm a great believer in positive thought."

She smiles sadly as Ivan pulls her close to his side and drops a light kiss on the top of her head.

"Come malyshka. I'm manifesting something in my own mind I need to make happen."

He grins as she rolls her eyes and, as they head off, Angelo laughs softly. I'll never grow tired of listening to them. Who guessed there was a woman out there who could tame the Savage?"

"Or the boss." I remind him of his own domestic bliss waiting at home, and he nods, looking a little pensive.

"What is it?" I'm seriously hoping there's not trouble in paradise, and he says with a gruff, "I owe you an apology."

"For what?"

"For telling you to stay away from my sister. I'm guessing you ignored that request anyway, but I just want you to know that if this all works out, I couldn't ask for a better brother-in-law and husband for her."

I can't even answer him because that must have been hard to say and as we hug it out, I battle my emotions once again because if I get the chance to pick up where I left off with Winter, I would be the luckiest bastard in the world.

CHAPTER 10

WINTER

It's as if I'm waking from the deepest dream. My mind floats in and out of consciousness and my limbs are heavy and ache. It's difficult to make out shapes, and the light hurts my eyes if I open them.

I hear voices, but they could be outside. I'm not sure where I am even. Am I still dreaming? I must be because like most dreams, nothing is making sense.

Am I floating above my body? Perhaps I am because something doesn't seem right.

I open my mouth to call someone, but I don't know their names. While I think about it, I don't even remember my name. Yes, it's a dream. I'll wake up and everything will be fine.

Once again, sleep takes me away from the scary place, but the next time I wake I'm still here. Is this a recurring dream? It must be, so I run with it. I have no control anyway, an emotion that hits me more than anything.

I have no control.

It bounces around my mind like an echo, telling me that wherever I am, it's because somebody told me to be here. I can't think for myself. That voice in my head is telling me not to make a fuss. You have no say in how you live your life. It's in somebody else's hands.

As my eyes flicker, I make out shapes all around me. Then I register two black shapes that are different to the rest.

I hear voices, deep, angry, hopeful voices, that appear to be shouting. They are loud, urgent and firm. *'Listen to them'*, my inner voice says. *'Do what they say at all times'.*

I struggle to open my eyes and as I do, the shapes come into focus, and I'm alarmed to find I can't move. Something is pinning me down and my first reaction is to scream, but nothing comes out. A silent scream. Is this part of the dream?

A rough hand strokes my face, and a husky voice whispers, "It's Alessandro, baby, you're safe now."

Another voice interrupts, "It's Angelo, talk to me."

I don't understand them. Who are they?

The noise increases and the shapes leave, but they are replaced by different ones, all calling out with an urgency that scares me a little.

I am touched, somebody is touching me, and I flinch as if it burns. My heart is thumping, I'm in danger, I must run. They want to hurt me.

I make to move, and somebody holds me down. I try to fight, but then they float away again on a cloud, leaving me back in blissful solitude.

It seems like days but could be seconds when I visit that place again. They're here, controlling me, making me do what they want. I'm a prisoner, I must escape. I can't think of anything else and as I struggle to open my eyes, I'm aware that I'm crying. I don't cry, I can't cry. Why am I crying?

Once again, I am held down on either side and I try to snatch my hands away from the strong ones holding me.

"Stop fighting. You're safe now." The deep voice to my right sounds angry.

"Please baby, you're safe. Nothing will hurt you."

The voice to my left says.

"Let me go." Somehow my voice quivers on the edge of the conversation and it doesn't sound like me. Then again, how do I know what I sound like because who am I, anyway?

Suddenly, my hands are released, and I feel victorious. I'm free. I'm allowed to leave.

A huge smile breaks out across my face and then I detect urgent whispers and strange sounds—machines, I'm guessing. What is this place?

Then another voice floats out of the fog. A kind, gentle voice, full of compassion. "My name is Doctor Carmichael. You're in the hospital."

"Am I sick?" My voice quivers with uncertainty, almost as if I forgot I had one.

"We don't know. We need you to wake up so we can assess you."

"I'm awake." If I could, I'd roll my eyes because can't he see that? We're having a conversation, aren't we?

The silence calms me and gives me the courage to open my eyes a little. Have they gone? Am I alone again? It's safer that way.

The room swims into focus, and I see a concerned pair of eyes staring into mine. He seems kind. I like that. He makes me feel safe, so I smile shyly.

"Do you remember your name?" He asks a dumb question that makes me laugh. "Of course."

"Tell me."

"It's…"

I stop because what the fuck is my name?

"It's…" I search for it in my memory, but it's gone. Where the fuck is my memory? There's nothing there.

'It's…" The tears roll down my face and the doctor looks to someone on my right and says quickly, "Tell her your name, it may trigger the memory."

I look to my right and the face staring back at me scares me a little. It's a man. A dark-haired man with the blackest eyes. He looks worried, angry, and powerful. He scares me a little.

"I'm Angelo, your brother. Your twin brother."

He seems upset about that and I shake my head. "I'd remember if I had a brother. You must be mistaking me for somebody else."

I try to ignore the pain in his eyes because I feel responsible for putting it there. He doesn't deserve pain. I don't either, but something is telling me I have a lot of pain in my life.

He looks to the person on my left and I swing my gaze to take a look and my heart skips a beat because this man is terrifying.

"I'm Alessandro, your…" He hesitates and then says slightly huskily, "Your friend."

"My friend."

I roll the word around my mind, hoping it connects with something. Do I have friends? I'm not sure, and the doctor says eagerly, "Do you remember anything at all?"

"No." I hang my head because I don't. A lone tear escapes, which somehow frightens me. I can't cry, please don't cry.

I can sense the disappointment in the room and close my eyes, waiting to be punished. Why am I waiting to be punished?

The doctor sighs and nods toward the door and the two men leave, even though I can tell it's the last thing they want to do.

As the door closes behind them, the doctor sits on the bed and takes my hand in his.

"You were involved in an accident where you hit your head. Can you remember anything at all about that?"

"No." I'm so stupid. I've let them all down. They will punish me.

The doctor sighs. "Your name is Winter Delauren, previously Sontauro. One of the men outside is your twin brother, Angelo."

None of this makes sense and I say miserably, "I'm sorry. I don't remember."

He nods and smiles kindly. "It's fine. Just get some rest and try not to think about it. Your memory will return, I'm sure. Blows to the head can trigger memory loss. It's probable it's short term and so enjoy the peace and quiet while you can."

He winks and heads to the door and I say in a whisper, "Am I in trouble?"

He looks surprised. "No, why?"

"You mean you won't punish me."

Now he just looks uncomfortable. "Of course not. Like your friend said, you're safe here."

"My friend. Alessandro."

He nods. I'm strangely comforted that I have a friend at least and I sigh and close my eyes, hearing the click of the door on his way out. I have a brother and a friend but why does it feel as if something important is missing?

CHAPTER 11

ALESSANDRO

*A*ngelo looks as if Winter just stabbed him in the heart and I'm feeling the same.

"That fucking bastard! What has he done to my sister?"

The anger sizzles around him like a lit trail of dynamite. "She's lost her memory. It's obvious the blow to her head caused it."

"Are you certain of that?"

Angelo growls. "What if that bastard did this? We don't know, we haven't spoken for over a year, if not longer. How do we know what hell he put her through?"

I fall silent because he has a point. None of us can possibly comprehend what Winter has been through and this could be Massimo's work. I wouldn't put it past him.

"We must pray she gets her memory back." I say with a sigh. "She's in the right place for that."

The doctor heads outside and shakes his head as we crowd around him.

"She's lost her memory; it's quite common in head trauma cases and may take a few days or weeks to return. We'll keep her in for a few days and run some tests, but she'll need your help."

"Name it."

I interrupt because I will do anything to bring her back to us.

"Talk about happy times. Her past, memories you share. Remind her who she is, and it may spark a memory. When she leaves, take her to familiar places. They may trigger them. It could be a long road and parts of it may never return, but she needs help."

"She'll have the best help there is."

Angelo grinds out in a firm voice and the doctor sighs again. "Just take it easy on her. Which brings me to a question I must ask."

"What question?"

I look at him hard and he shrinks a little. "She thinks she's in trouble and will be punished. Is there anything you can tell me about that?"

It's possible Angelo is about to tear this hospital apart with his bare hands as he growls, "The fucking bastard."

The doctor looks worried, and I say angrily, "It's her husband. You'll find the term is domestic abuse."

The doctor nods. "I see. Where is her husband now?"

We both nod and say in unison, "In hell doctor, her husband is in hell."

To his credit, he just smiles and nods toward Winter's room. "Then I'll leave her in your capable hands. I'm guessing it explains the bruising to her face and throat. Maybe I should report this to the cops."

His voice trails off as we fix him with our darkest looks and Angelo growls, "No cops. It's been dealt with."

The doctor edges away and clears his throat. "Of course, well, as I said, we'll monitor the situation, but I expect she'll be discharged in a few days with, or without her memory."

As he heads off, Angelo turns to face me with Satan's fury blazing from his eyes and spits, "Massimo had better still be alive because I want to murder the fucking bastard ten times over."

"I'll get an update from my grandfather. I'll tell him to keep him warm until we get there."

Angelo nods. "The most important thing right now is my sister. We'll take it in shifts watching her. I'm trusting no one else."

"I'm not leaving her."

"And you think I want to?"

He stares at me with a hard expression that I throw right back at him, causing us both to grin at the same time.

"Fine." He throws up his hands. "I'll head back to Jasmine and fill her in. Get her to pack a few things for Winter and then you can head off and grab some sleep."

"I'm staying."

He rolls his eyes. "Then I'll get her to pack a bag for you, too."

He heads back into Winter's room, and I give them a moment because I understand his claim on her is far greater than mine.

As I wander to the vending machine, I select a coffee and wait, pulling out my phone to check my texts. The first one is from my grandfather.

Call me when you have news. The visitor is settling into his new home. Brief me on your expectations.

Picturing the treatment my grandfather probably inflicted on our guest gives me a moment's satisfaction and I dash off a quick reply.

What state is he in?

I HOPE he's conscious at least, only to prolong his suffering.

I'm not sure what was in that injection, but he's paralyzed. The doctor checked him over and believes he had a stroke. His vital signs are good, and he responds with his eyes, so his brain is functioning. Relax in the knowledge, he's going nowhere. How is your woman?

A simple question that there is no answer for. Firstly, I don't know how she is and secondly, she may never agree to be my woman, so I type,

Alive.

The next text is from Flynn.

Fucking update me, you bastard. What's happening? I'm out of my freaking mind here.

I tap back.

You're always out of your freaking mind, you nutjob. Winter's alive but lost her memory. She suffered a nasty blow to her head on the way down. The only good thing about that is she can't remember what an asshole you are.

The third is from Malik.

There is currently a specialist on standby and can arrange transport to the best hospital in the world for Winter. Tell me when I can proceed.

> **Thanks man, but it's ok for now. She may need some help when we leave the hospital. I'll keep you updated. She's lost her memory, but otherwise all seems fine. She injected Massimo with something. Find out who picked that up because we need to discover what it contained.**

As I shut off my phone, I grab the coffee and head back, hating the fact she was out of my sight for five minutes already.

* * *

As soon as I return, Angelo heads out and I offer him a swig of the disgusting hospital coffee.

"Is this the best you can do? I need a fucking bottle of whiskey right now."

He takes a sip and shivers and I grin. "Not your preferred blend I take it."

"It's not even coffee." He growls and says wearily, "I'm heading off. I asked Winter what she needs, and I'll bring it back. I told her you would stay here to keep her company. Poor girl, as if she hasn't been through enough already, but it can't be helped."

His teasing tone lightens the mood a little because we were standing on a thin line back there, not knowing if she would wake up. The loss of memory in this case may be a blessing in disguise because the horrors she lived through are best forgotten if she wants to lead a happy life.

As he heads off, I take a moment before heading back to her side. I must think this through as I need Winter to remember what happened between us, because if she walks away from me again, I'm not sure I would survive.

CHAPTER 12

WINTER

Apparently, my name is Winter, which pissed me off. What kind of fucking stupid name is that? Why was I named after the most depressing season there is? Summer, I could live with, even Spring, although that just sounds plain stupid.

For the next two days, my friend doesn't leave my side. He's there when I wake and when I fall asleep. The man's a machine and as the shadow deepens on his jaw, I feel guilty that he's not getting the chance to sleep in his own bed and take a shower at least.

There is something about Alessandro that comforts me, and I haven't a clue why. He's a scary man in every way, from his dark eyes and wild hair that's tamed by a ponytail. The muscles that flex when he moves, and the ink scripted on his biceps that interests me way more than it should.

He has tried to help me by talking about a place called Rockwell Academy where apparently I went to college. I shared a house with him and my brother and four other people. I remember none of them.

He told me I married a man called Massimo against my will.

The hatred in his eyes told me they didn't get along and I wonder about that.

I still don't remember a thing.

Names are fired at me and places I've supposedly been, but nothing sounds familiar.

It's so frustrating, especially because it's obvious he wants me to remember so badly, which surprises me.

I love the soft way he smiles and the gentle touches he makes before pulling back when I shrink away. I can tell it hurts him, but I don't want to be touched. I can't explain it.

My brother returns and brings me clothes, make-up and magazines. There are flowers from names that mean nothing to me. There are so many they even spill out onto the ward outside. I have been allocated a private room apparently, which I'm happy about.

After a few more days, I am discharged and as I walk between the two men who have stayed with me throughout this whole experience, I'm nervous for a very different reason.

Where are we going? Do I have a home? Will I remember it when I'm there?

To my surprise, we are met outside the hospital by a fleet of black shiny cars. Men stand waiting like a guard of honor, dressed in black with dark shades covering their eyes.

I stare around me in shock and Alessandro whispers, "Relax, this is normal."

"For you maybe." I blink as I take it all in and as a man holds a door open for me, I'm almost afraid to step inside.

Alessandro sits beside me on one side and Angelo on the other and as the door slams and we follow the car in front, I whisper, "What's going on?"

Angelo takes my hand and squeezes it reassuringly. "The hospital told us we had to take you somewhere familiar."

"To my home."

"No."

"Then where?"

Angelo sighs heavily. "Unfortunately, your home has been destroyed and there is nothing left of it. The home we lived in as children has been rebuilt. There are no memories here that would trigger anything, so we have arranged for you to spend the next few months on vacation instead."

"Vacation?"

That was the last thing I expected to hear, and Alessandro takes my other hand and says softly, "To Italy. To my home."

"But why?"

He flinches a little and I see an emotion in his eyes that confuses me.

"Because you are safe there and because it's the perfect place to recuperate."

"Will you be coming too?" I stare hopefully at my brother, and he nods, the strangest expression flitting across his face.

"I will be there for a few days, no more. My wife will meet us at the airport, so you will have some female company to enjoy."

"Your wife? Do I know her?"

I can't believe what I'm hearing, and Angelo shakes his head. "No, you've only met once."

"Why?"

I'm so confused because why would I not be part of their lives if he's my twin brother?

"Does she hate me?" I'm almost afraid of the reply and Angelo shakes his head. "Of course not. Nobody could ever hate you."

"Then why does it feel as if I've done something wrong all the time?"

The men beside me tense and I wonder what they're not telling me. It's so hard trying to remember. I don't recognize anyone, not even myself, and I'm so alone. I'm hating every minute of it and yet something is telling me I'm safe with the two most scary men I have ever met. Not that I remember meeting any. It's as if I was born a few days ago in the hospital and have yet to live my life.

I'm surprised when we pull into a private airfield and see a sleek aircraft waiting. "What's this?"

I stare in awe and Alessandro shrugs. "My grandfather's jet."

"Wow, he must be very rich."

"He is."

The car door is wrenched open, and Alessandro exits first, and I hear a low, "Bueno sera, Alessandro."

"Bueno sera, Michele."

He reaches in and offers me his hand, but I don't take him up on the offer. I can tell he hates the fact I won't allow myself to be touched. Not by anyone, and I wonder about that. Have I always been so weird? I certainly hope not, but there is something very wrong about anyone's hands on me. Almost as if I would be punished for it. I don't understand why, and I wonder if it has anything to do with the man they said I married, Massimo.

As I head up the steps of the aircraft, I think about my wedding. I have no memory of it all. Was I in love and where is he now?

I'm so confused and when I step into the aircraft, I gaze around in wonder because I wasn't expecting this.

This isn't an aircraft; it's a hotel and I blink at the scale of this place. It's dripping with luxury and has comfy leather seats and stylish furniture, kitting out a palace with wings.

I'm in awe when a woman stands and heads toward us with a welcoming smile and I don't miss the fact my brother tears a path straight to her and takes her in his arms.

As they break away, she blushes as he pulls her forward and says proudly, "Winter, meet Jasmine, my wife."

She smiles and seems friendly enough as she says gently, "I'm pleased to see you again, Winter."

"Again?" I'm so confused because I have never met this woman before and her slightly startled expression is quickly covered as she smiles. "Come and take a seat. I'm here to answer any questions at all and reassure you that there are women in this man's world we inhabit."

She makes a valid point because it's as if their world is filled with men in black suits and so I'm grateful to slip into a seat beside her and accept the glass of champagne she hands me.

"To having you back where you belong."

She raises her glass and I say with a worried frown. "Why, where have I been?"

I don't miss the concerned look in her eye as she smiles sweetly. "It must be frightening losing your memory."

"It is." I shake my head. "There is so much I need to remember, well everything really and I can't believe I've forgotten my own name."

I take a sip of the cool champagne and she smiles. "Some rest and recuperation may jog your memory right back."

"I hope so."

As the men climb on board and take up two seats nearby, I steal a glance at my 'friend' Alessandro. There is something so magnificent about him that has made my interest grow over the past few days. He is a gentle giant and there is something so comforting being around him, not to mention that I find him incredibly sexy.

Jasmine obviously notices me staring and laughs softly. "He's very handsome."

"He is." I hate the desperation in my voice as I long for more than just friendship with this man, but I'm in no position to want something that can never be mine. I'm married anyway, so surely my husband must be worried about me.

"Will my husband be there?" I'm curious about that, and Jasmine's startled reaction tells me I'm not going to like her answer.

"I… I… um, don't think so."

She is struggling and I wonder about that. There is something they aren't telling me and so I call out to my brother.

"Where is my husband?"

The silence fills the plane, telling me I'm not going to like this, and the expression on his face scares me a little as he growls, "Hopefully in hell."

"I don't understand."

I'm stunned and even more afraid when he spits, "That bastard was no husband to you. He was a bully who made your life a living hell. You will never see him again."

I flinch at his words and Jasmine says quickly, "What Angelo means is that you were divorcing him. He wasn't a nice man and, well, you're better off not remembering anything about him."

"I was divorcing him. Why?"

I can't believe I don't remember that, and Angelo says bitterly, "Because he is the man responsible for putting you in hospital."

As the engines start up, it takes our attention away from the conversation and as we taxi out, I lean back in my seat with a troubled feeling inside. Whatever happened between me and my husband wasn't good it seems and yet surely I would remember that. Remember him even.

Once again, I steal a look at Alessandro and take a sharp breath because the fury on his face tells me he's angry about this. What did my husband do and why do they hate him so much?

As the plane takes off to God only knows where, I pray so hard that my memory is waiting for me there because something important is tapping away inside me. Something I must remember, and I don't have a clue what it is.

CHAPTER 13

ALESSANDRO

All this time, I've wanted Winter back. It's been the most important thing on my mind and the driving force behind everything I do. Now she's here, I must deal with my emotions. I never thought for one second she wouldn't remember me. I understand it's due to the head wound, but it's killing me inside.

As I watch her from the corner of my eye as she chats with Jasmine, I physically ache to touch her. To pull her beside me and hold on tight because I love her. I have no doubt about that, but I'm a stranger to her. She is polite, but the lost expression in her eyes is tearing me apart and I'm not alone. Angelo is also going through hell because she may be here physically, but mentally, she is fucked.

Was it something Massimo did, and the head wound had no part in this? I need answers and so does the boss, which is why we decided it was best to take her to Sicily.

Just picturing the man responsible, currently residing in my grandfather's holding cell, makes my blood sizzle like flesh on fire. We have business to attend to in Sicily. Mafia business and they don't call me The Beast for nothing.

Angelo leans forward and says in a low voice, "Under no circumstances is Winter ever to see that bastard again. Keep her well away from him."

"Do you really think I'd allow that?" I fix him with a bitter expression. "That bastard will regret the day he took Winter from us."

Angelo nods, the hatred glittering behind his eyes. "Will she be ok?"

He looks worried and I snap. "Yes. She will come back to us. Part of me hopes her memory never returns, and she never has to live with what that bastard did to her. But we want our girl back and I will do everything possible to make that happen."

We both glance over and see Winter lying back against the seat, her eyes closed. Jasmine flashes Angelo a concerned look, and he sighs. "I never thought it would be like this."

As I stare at the beauty who stars in my dreams every night, I nod with bitter agreement. "I certainly never expected it."

Sighing, I bring the conversation back to business.

"What happened at Massimo's mansion?"

"Fucking weirdo." Angelo shakes his head.

"Why?"

"The place was impenetrable. Even the fact his men had left didn't help us. The place is protected by weird biometric shit. We couldn't even kick the doors or window in."

"So, what did you do?"

I'm curious and he shrugs. "We blew it to fucking hell."

"Is there anything left?"

"I fucking hope not."

He laughs softly. "It's a building plot. Apparently, the news reports are writing it off as a freak gas explosion. Fire crews attempted to save it, but all that's left is dust."

"Any casualties?" I'm mildly interested, and he shakes his head.

"Not reported ones, but who knows what poor unfortunate souls were held in that house of horrors?"

"Could it come back on you?"

"What do you think?"

"What about Flynn? Have you heard back from him?"

"Same. Everything's gone. It was a consolidated attack that even if Massimo had survived Scarpetta, he would have nothing to return to. His men had deserted him, and his real estate torched. We took everything from him except his life, it seems."

"Are you blaming me for that?"

I fix him with my deadliest stare, and he says bitterly, "Of course not. Nobody expected Winter to take matters into her own hands. If only she'd known your gun was trained on the back of his head, she wouldn't have damaged hers."

I cast my mind back to the moment I almost pulled the trigger. The exact second, she moved by his side, and it could so easily have been her body we dragged from the restaurant. Just the thought of it tears me apart and I reach for the whiskey and drain the glass in seconds.

"Keep a clear head. We have business to attend to."

Angelo snaps and I pointedly ignore him and refill my glass. Sighing, he stands and whispers angrily, "We've got what we wanted. Winter's alive, and it's only a matter of time before she regains her memory. I'm sure none of us are prepared for that."

He heads off and beckons his wife to follow him, and I stare at the seat she vacated and feel the magnetic pull. Standing, I take her seat and stare with a hunger at the woman who appears to be sleeping. She looks so perfect, so beautiful, like a rose that has been scratched by one of its own thorns. Part broken but still the most beautiful thing I have ever seen and despite being so fragile, she has a strength that will cause her to bloom once more.

Her eyes open and I glance away, conscious I may be

scaring her. I understand I'm not your average Joe and scare the fuck out of most people who catch my eye, but I want a different kind of look from this woman beside me.

She smiles shyly and I swear it melts my heart and my expression softens as I say huskily, "I'm sorry to wake you."

"I wasn't really sleeping, just resting my eyes."

I note the dark circles under her eyes despite her extended sleep in the hospital and I'm concerned that we are moving too fast.

"Did they give you any medication? Are you feeling sick?"

She shakes her head. "Just painkillers, but I'm guessing they're wearing off."

"Show them to me."

She reaches into her purse, and I grasp a bottle of water nearby and tear off the cap, offering it to her with a soft, "Drink the lot. It will help."

"Thank you doctor."

She giggles and I swear it's the sweetest sound in the world and it actually pastes a smile on my own angry face.

"That's better."

"What is?" I'm not sure what she means, and she whispers, "It's good to see you smiling."

"I have something to smile about now."

"What?"

"You, Winter. You're back where you belong."

"Why did I leave?" She's curious and yet I'm not sure if she could cope with the truth and I sigh, aching to grasp her hand and raise it to my lips. "Let's just say your husband wasn't the most sociable person in the world."

"My husband."

She looks worried.

"I should remember I had a husband. Where is he now?"

"Somewhere he can't hurt you."

Her eyes widen and I say with a deep sigh. "To be honest,

you are best forgetting all about him. He's not worth your effort. Concentrate on remembering who Winter is and take it from there."

"What about you?"

She gazes at me with a curious smile. "You say we're friends. Where did we meet?"

"Rockwell Academy. Don't you remember we spoke about it at the hospital?"

"We did?" She looks surprised and the warning bells start ringing loud and clear.

"It was only a couple of days ago."

"I'm sorry." She looks upset.

"What for?"

"Not recalling our conversation."

"Do you remember the hospital?"

"Yes, but, well…"

"Well, what?"

"I remember I was there."

Suddenly, her eyes fill with tears and the agony on her face is too much to bear, especially when she whispers, "I'm frightened, Alessandro."

Fuck convention and in one swift move I pull her into my arms and hold her so tightly the emotion almost breaks me. As I pull her frail body in my arms, it's like a homecoming. Her gentle sobs slices open my heart and as I stroke her hair and whisper words of reassurance, it would take a bullet through my head to release her now. I can't let go. Finally, she is where she belongs and yet she's broken. Can we repair her? You can bet your fucking life we can, even if we engage every specialist in the world. Winter is in the safest hands and whatever she needs, she will get.

When Angelo and Jasmine return, I make no move to release Winter from my arms. Angelo looks destroyed when he sees her sobbing gently into my chest and Jasmine brushes a tear from her eye. I shake my head and continue stroking her hair because this is what she needs right now. She must feel so alone and there is no need for that. She will never be alone again, even if I make it my life's work.

Angelo says gently, "Winter, can I get you anything?"

His voice causes her to glance up, and she smiles through her tears. "I'm so sorry. I don't know what came over me. I don't suppose you have a glass of water."

Jasmine grabs one from the refrigerator and hands it to her and, as she sips the cool liquid, she settles into my arms as if she was always meant to be there.

She looks up from under her lashes and says in a whisper, "Thank you."

"No need. I will always be here for you."

"I guess that's because you're my friend. I can see why I like you."

I tighten my grip and swallow the rush of words I really want to say and as she sips her water, she closes her eyes and makes no effort to move.

As we carry on our journey to Sicily, all my dreams have come true. My woman is back in my arms, but fate's a complicated bitch and I wonder how long I get to keep her there.

CHAPTER 14

WINTER

I should have thanked him and taken my seat again. I don't know why, but I couldn't leave his arms if I tried. There is something so comforting about them. As if I have a home here. The fact he makes my pulse race, and my heart flutter, may have something to do with it because this man was crafted from my dreams. He seems so familiar to me and I'm guessing it's because he's my friend, but for some reason I want more.

As we take the flight, I am in no hurry to move, and I settle down with his arms locked around me and fall asleep. This time there are no nightmares. I'm safe here. It doesn't even seem wrong, as if I will be punished for doing something I shouldn't. No, with Alessandro there are no threats, no bad feelings, only happiness.

It's dark when we touch down in Sicily and it's as if I've been traveling for days. We all appear to be tired, and I wonder about the place we're heading. I don't think I've ever been to Italy, but they will probably tell me I live here. It's the strangest experience not knowing my history. There is a fog where my memory used to be. I can sense it. A barrier against information, and I'm hoping a few more days may change everything.

Once again, we travel in convoy. I chose to go with Alessandro because Angelo would probably prefer to travel with his wife. I still don't understand why I've never met her before. I must be the worst sister in the world, and I hate my past self already.

Alessandro seems on edge, but I can't fault his attention to me. He fussed around me the entire flight and it was quite sweet, really.

Even in the car, he pulled me tenderly against his shoulder, allowing my head to rest on it and it felt so natural.

As we head toward his home, I say tentatively, "What happens now?"

"You rest." His soft reply makes me smile because I am fast learning I love hearing him speak. It's slightly rough with a husky edge and sounds incredibly sexy on him.

"Do you have a girlfriend?" I blush as my thoughts turn into words that came from nowhere and he says gently, "No."

"Why not?"

"Because my heart belongs to only one woman and always has."

"Oh." I'm crushed for some reason, disappointed even and suddenly wonder if I should be as close to him as I am. He must be hating every minute of this and is only being kind because he's my friend.

I make to pull away and he growls, "Stay where you are."

"But ..."

"I said, stay where you are."

"Why?"

I hold my breath as he whispers, "Because it's where you belong."

Tears well in my eyes at the slightly desperate tone of his voice and as I snuggle in a little closer, I whisper, "This woman.

Where is she now?" He hesitates slightly before saying, "Fuck this."

"Excuse me."

I'm shocked when he shrugs me off and turns to face me and I gasp when I see the passion flashing in his eyes. He looks angry for some reason, and I wonder why and then he grasps my face in both his hands so gently as if he's afraid I'll break and whispers, "She's right here, Winter. The only woman I have ever loved and ever will is you."

"Me?" I'm lost for words, and he says with a tortured breath, "I lost you once, but I'll be damned if I let it happen again. You were taken from me and given to another, and I have spent two fucking years trying to get you back. The fact you don't remember tears a hole in my soul, but you will remember and if you don't…"

He breaks off and whispers, "I'll make you fall in love with me all over again."

"You love me." I'm shocked at the powerful emotion in his eyes and he whispers, his lips grazing against mine, "I will always love you, Winter, and one day I hope you will love me right back."

He pulls away and slings his arm around my shoulder and says gruffly, "No more talking. I've said enough."

As the car continues down the road, something shifts inside me. Hope, happiness and desire, all wrapped up in anxiety. Did I love him too? Then why did I marry somebody else? Is he telling me the truth? I'm not sure of anything anymore and so I close my eyes and pray that when I open them again, it's with my memory back because I'm lost without it and don't know who or what to believe.

* * *

We make the rest of the journey in silence and as we turn off the slightly bumpy road, I see huge iron gates barring our entrance and watch in surprise when they swing open, allowing the entourage to pass through. I'm not sure who these people are, and I may have lost my memory, but I'm not stupid and I shiver when I contemplate what's happening here. The dark suits, the convoy, the private plane, and the rough edges of the men can only mean one thing—Mafia.

Don't ask me how I know, I just do. It's the one certainty in a life with none. I think deep down I've always known, which gives me hope that one day the rest of the picture will be revealed. I wonder what that makes Alessandro and Angelo. Do they work for the man in charge? Are they soldiers, or more?

As we sweep through the gates, I look out on the shadows because the sky is as black as Satan's heart and our progress is only illuminated by the lighting that lines the driveway. I make out a huge shape in front of us, which I'm guessing is the house, and it takes forever to navigate the path up to it.

Alessandro is tense. I can sense he changed the moment we swept through the gates, and I wonder about that. Is he in trouble for bringing me here? I am a married woman, after all. Will my husband be angry? Did they kidnap me? He told me he had been trying to get me back for two years. Will my husband come for me? Will he hurt Alessandro?

I have so many questions but no fucking answers and if I didn't have a headache before, I do now.

The car stops and the door is wrenched opened and suddenly I'm scared. Everything appears so dark, so threatening and as Alessandro's hand reaches for mine, I grasp it like a lifeline, intending on not letting go.

We follow the soldiers inside the house and as they melt into the shadows, I see a woman waiting, looking at us with curiosity. She has a hard edge to her, sharp eyes and patrician features that soften when Alessandro steps forward and says respectfully, "Nonna."

He drops my hand and embraces her and as they kiss on both cheeks, I'm mesmerized. Despite her severe welcome, I can tell she is respected here and as Alessandro steps back to my side, he immediately takes my hand again and says with a slight edge to his voice, "This is Winter."

Nonna looks at me intently, and I feel her razor-sharp stare penetrating through my defensive layers. I'm almost positive she knows everything about me from one lingering look and then she steps forward and, to my surprise, pulls me in for a hug.

"Mio bellissimo angelo, Benvenuto."

I'm not sure what she even says, but Alessandro laughs softly and says, "I couldn't have said that better myself."

As she releases me, I whisper, "What did she say?"

He squeezes my hand. "She said, welcome home."

He must sense my confusion, because he grips my hand a little tighter. "You can ask me anything, but not now. You're to go with Nonna and Jasmine. We have business to discuss."

"You're leaving me."

I'm worried about that, and he pulls me closer and whispers, "Not for long. I'll be back as quick as I can. Don't worry, you are safer here than anyone and Jasmine will be right by your side."

Jasmine steps forward and reaches for my hand.

"Come, Winter. Nonna has arranged coffee, or something stronger if you prefer."

As we follow Nonna to what I'm assuming will be the kitchen, I glance back and see Alessandro watching me leave with those dark, sexy eyes, glittering with something that should scare me but for some reason only makes me impatient for him to return.

CHAPTER 15

ALESSANDRO

The fact Winter is in my family home is surprisingly comforting. When I first fell in love with her, this is the last place I wanted to bring her, but after everything that's happened, it's the only place I can be certain she's safe. My home is everything you would expect from one that has spent centuries controlling crime. Riches steeped in history and old money that funds a new modern life.

As Angelo walks beside me, I can tell he's deep in thought and so am I. Leaving Winter was hard because she is the only thing that occupies my thoughts and has done since she was taken. Now she's back, I'm not certain of our future except for one thing. Hers is with me if I spend the rest of my life trying.

Angelo says in his deep voice, "Your home is impressive."

"I suppose."

I gaze around me dismissively because it's a sight I'm used to, having grown up here for the best part of my life. When my father left, I stayed and was only given my freedom to attend Rockwell Academy, where I met my friends. I wonder if my grandfather regrets that decision now.

I can tell Angelo has something he wants to say because the

silence is an unnatural one and so I guide him into a different room than the one we are heading for. As we walk into the living room, the heavy drapes conceal the magnificent gardens outside and the dim lamplight creates drama where it definitely isn't needed.

I head across to the table by the window where a decanter of whiskey resides and pour us two glasses, nodding toward the couch.

"Whatever's on your mind, say it before we meet with my grandfather."

Angelo nods, taking the glass from my hand and facing me with a contemplative expression.

"It's Winter."

"I guessed as much."

I face him with a brooding stare, and he surprises me by saying with a sigh. "I want her to stay here with you."

"Why?" I'm surprised at that because Angelo is overly protective of his twin, and I always knew I would have a fight on my hands when he wanted to return home with her.

Sighing, he twists the tumbler of amber liquid in his hands and sighs heavily. "She needs stability. Our family home is different to the one that stood before it, and despite Jasmine's assurances that she will look after her, I believe it's a different sort of care she needs right now."

"Say it and it will be arranged."

His lips twist into a sardonic smile. "The type of care she needs is love, Alessandro."

"Love." I'm not sure I'm hearing him right, and he laughs softly. "I've seen the way she looks at you. Even with her memory on hold, she sees something in you that makes her happy. God knows why, but it's obvious."

He rolls his eyes. "I can tell she's comfortable around you and that's just what she needs right now. To relax and possibly open up to someone. Allow the bad memories to be crushed by new happy ones and I'm guessing you're the man for the job."

"The only man." I growl and he shakes his head. "Just take care of her and keep me updated. Bring her back to us, that's all I ask."

For some reason, his words make me emotional because earning his acceptance of the situation means more than he will ever realize. Angelo isn't just one of my closest friends, he's like a brother to me. They all are and entrusting me with his precious twin is the greatest gift he could ever gift me.

"I won't let you down."

My voice is rough and outlined in emotion and his dark, glittering eyes fix on me with a turbulent warning.

"She's my only blood, Alessandro. She's all I've got. Bring her back."

I nod and swallow hard because I don't want him to see how weak this is making me. I need to be strong and powerful to cope with the possibility Winter may never recover from the trauma of the past few years. Whatever Massimo did to her has had a devastating effect and as my thoughts turn to the monster currently wounded, but not dead, I growl ominously, "We have a visit to make."

Angelo nods and I see the darkness swirl around him like the deadliest storm about to break and as we stand, we do so with one aim in mind. To make Massimo Delauren pay for his crimes against our family.

* * *

We head to my grandfather's den, where he is waiting to fill us in. The ever-present soldiers are positioned at every turn, watching us move past with dark curiosity. They know I am the Don's heir and I command a certain respect, but even I understand I must earn that if I am ever to gain their loyalty.

They respect my grandfather through past actions and he has lived a long and vengeful life because he is always one step ahead of his enemies and the soldiers who serve him hold a deep love for him. He treats them well and yet is hard and cruel when it counts, and I've learned a lot from him over the years.

As we stop outside his den, I take a deep breath and then nod to the soldier guarding the door and as he opens it, the scent of cigar smoke and brandy reaches out and draws me into the familiar.

"Alessandro." My grandfather's low, deep voice calls me in, and I move to his side and embrace him as expected. I kiss him on both cheeks, as is customary and he nods his approval and gestures to one of two seats placed opposite his own. Angelo approaches and shakes his hand, and I can tell my friend has his respect as he says, "Don Sontauro, I am honored to welcome you to my home."

"Don Majerio, I am your loyal servant and must thank you from the bottom of my heart for bringing my sister home."

My grandfather nods, a contemplative glint in his eye, and as Angelo takes the seat beside me, he hands us both a glass of his favorite poison.

"Then we drink to a strong alliance."

We raise our glasses and, as we drain them, I wonder what he has in mind. We both owe him our souls and knowing my grandfather, he will enjoy possessing them and will waste no time in calling in the favor.

"Massimo." My grandfather shakes his head. "The madness was distressing to watch. Portia was right to bring it to my attention."

Thinking of my grandfather's mistress, I'm still queasy about the whole set up and the twinkle in his eye doesn't make me feel any better as he says with pleasure, "An enjoyable trip that was cut short. I won't leave my return one so long."

He laughs at the disgust on my face and whispers, "Don't

judge me because until you walk in a man's shoes, you haven't earned the right. Maybe one day you will tread the same path. Many of our ancestors learned the lesson and realized the importance of options."

Like my friend beside me, I have zero intentions of that and just nod politely to bring an end to this disturbing conversation. My grandfather sighs heavily. "I am happy to welcome Winter back into the family. I am guessing she will *be* family, given the lengths my grandson has gone to." He looks slyly at Angelo, probably to gauge his reaction, and my friend just nods and says firmly, "I would be honored if Winter was welcomed into such a fine family as the Majerio one."

My grandfather puffs on his cigar and appears to be in a thoughtful mood and I say hastily, "You have something we want."

As he blows out the smoke rings, he chuckles. "I wondered how long it would take you. I expected you to be eager to play with our new guest."

"Where is he?"

"Under lock and key, although his accommodation is not as salubrious as the one your friend here will enjoy."

"Can we see him?"

Angelo is as desperate as I am, and my grandfather nods.

"Of course. Allow me to accompany you."

I stare at him in surprise because my grandfather doesn't usually get involved in the hard stuff anymore. He prefers to let his enforcers earn their generous pay, but I'm guessing, as always, he's testing me, ensuring I'm capable of taking the top job and making him proud.

As we follow him through the double doors that lead out onto the terrace, I take a deep breath of Sicilian air. It always calms my raging thoughts because my homeland may be turbulent and unforgiving, steeped in retribution and sinister dealings, but it's always been a place I love with all my heart.

Sicily runs through my veins and is a possessive bitch. She owns my soul and keeps me grounded and is the woman who scripted my life plan. I belong here, I always have and yet I wanted more. I wanted it all. To be free of the shit that makes up my DNA and try to live a normal life. I was a fool. This is normal life—to me, anyway, and I see that clearly. Now Winter is by my side, I know this is our home. It felt so right bringing her here, and as soon as we stepped inside, the realization hit me hard. America may be my second love, but Sicily will always be my first, and I belong here. I always did.

CHAPTER 16

WINTER

I am overawed by everything that's happened, but this house and this woman have stunned me. It's as if history is seeping from the walls and reaching out to pull me in. Whispers from the past accompany me along the impressive corridors as we follow silently behind a queen. The regal way she glides rather than walks tells me she's a powerful force in this world.

Jasmine is nervous beside me, and I wonder about that. Maybe she can also sense the importance of this occasion. As we follow Nonna into a huge kitchen, I feel immediately at home in the warm and welcoming space.

A maid stands to attention, apparently shocked by the invasion and almost bows as Nonna snaps, "Maria, i miei ospiti hanno bisogno di un rinfresco. Lo prenderemo al tavolo."

I'm not sure what she says, but the maid nods and scurries to the huge range cooker as Nonna points to the chairs set around a marble-topped table. "Excuse the informality, but sometimes a good dose of homeliness is what's needed after a hard journey."

"Thank you." Jasmine sounds grateful about that, and I nod in agreement. "It's so kind of you."

Nonna raises her eyes. "One thing you should realize, my angel, is that I am not kind." She laughs softly. "I am a mafia wife and kindness has no place in my world. Duty is the driving force and an acceptance of the situation, but one thing you should both learn and fast is that kindness gets you nowhere."

I'm shocked and a little worried about that and I'm guessing Jasmine is too, because she catches my eye and smiles tentatively. Probably now isn't the time to call Nonna out on that, so we just nod meekly and take our seats, just grateful to sit down.

Nonna sits opposite and her sharp expression makes me a little uncomfortable and then she addresses Jasmine. "You are married to a don. Does he treat you well?"

"Very well." The slight smile on Jasmine's face settles my heart. At least my brother loves her. It's obvious by the sparkle in her eyes and Nonna sighs. "Young love, I had that once."

She shakes her head. "It took a while to grow because mine was an arranged marriage and at the beginning, I fought the decision."

This is interesting and I can sense Jasmine is as fascinated as I am as Nonna leans forward and the devilish glint in her eyes makes us both smile.

"I soon learned the power of a woman over even the strongest man, and when I wielded it, I brought him to his knees. If you like, I can educate you both, but I'm guessing you don't need any pointers from an old and weary woman like myself."

We make to disagree, and she laughs out loud.

"It's fine. You don't need my help. I already see two men who will do anything to place the happiness in your eyes. I just hope you are strong enough to deal with what happens when that light fades and they move on to the next in line."

I'm not sure of the point of this conversation because I am already married and, according to Alessandro, my light died years ago and so I say tentatively, "Do you know my husband?"

It's as if Voldemort is in the room because both women appear nervous and glance around them fearfully.

Jasmine reaches for my hand and Nonna sighs heavily. "Your husband is a dead man."

"He's dead." I blink in disbelief, because how did I not know this?

Jasmine reaches across and squeezes my hand reassuringly as Nonna says harshly, "I understand you have lost your memory. Be prepared because when it returns, you may not like what you discover."

She stares at me with a very hard glare. "You have been brought here to start again. My grandson is infatuated with you. He has sacrificed a great deal to set you free from your life, and you should be grateful for that."

Jasmine says tentatively, "I don't think now is…"

"Now is the perfect time." Nonna peers across the table and her stone, cold stare unnerves me—a lot.

"Alessandro will be the Don of the Majerio family. It's a title that bears great responsibility. He will need to marry well, and another man's cast offs are not acceptable considering his position."

"I really must…" Jasmine speaks up bravely, but Nonna holds up her hand and says harshly, "A mafia bride must be a virgin on her wedding night. The fact you've been married before, my dear Winter, that means you are not. So, I ask you one thing."

"Which is?" I can guess what's coming as she sighs and leans forward, staring deep into my eyes. "Don't get too close. Resist him for his own sake. As I said before, choosing a mafia wife is a business decision. Nothing less. Marriage for power and a bride who will devote her entire life to continuing the line."

"I disagree."

Jasmine speaks up and appears angry. "I love my husband and he loves me. We are happy."

"Was it arranged? Did he marry you for what your family could give him?" Nonna leans forward with interest as Jasmine looks away and says in a weaker voice. "Yes, but…"

"But nothing. I rest my case. I'm also guessing you were a virgin on your wedding night."

Jasmine looks down and Nonna says triumphantly, "You must know that Alessandro will do whatever it takes to make you fall in love with him. I am asking you not to for his own good. He will be seen as weak among our enemies and a fool. If he takes another man's wife, soiled goods, as they say, it will be seen as bad business. I'm sorry to be direct, but I must lay my cards on the table at the beginning before it's too late."

I'm not sure how I answer her, but I do, and I gather all my dignity around me and say firmly, "Your request has been noted, but you forget one thing."

"I doubt it but continue."

"I may have lost my memory, but I'm not stupid. Firstly, I am in no position to start anything with another man when I don't even remember my husband. For all I know, we were in love and happy and he is out there looking for me. You say he's dead…" I fix her with my own hard glare and snap, "Why should I believe you? I've never met any of you and you could be playing me for a fool. So, in answer to your question, I didn't ask to be brought here. I don't remember your grandson, not really, and as for falling in love and marrying into this family, I'll pass on another wedding before I discover what happened to my husband. But one thing you should understand, Mrs. Majerio…"

"Go on." Nonna regards me with interest as I hiss, "If I did fall in love with Alessandro, I wouldn't let tradition get in the way of that. The life you speak of is cold and unfeeling, but I want more than that. I don't want to be a mafia wife locked in an emotionally retarded contract just to produce the next cold-blooded killer, so if anything, I pity you making that your life's work."

I am fuming with anger. How dare she warn me off something that isn't even a thing, anyway. The soft laugh beside me tells me Jasmine agrees, and I'm surprised to witness a twinkle in the eye of the woman who riled me up.

"Well said, Winter. I can see why my grandson wants you. Just consider what I said. It will become clearer the longer you spend here. You will discover how life works in Sicily and conclude I'm right. It's nothing personal, my dear, just business. I hope you understand."

She stands and says pleasantly, "Allow me to show you both to your respective rooms. I'm guessing you would like to freshen up, or possibly take an early night. Tomorrow will be a brighter day for everyone and Winter…"

She smiles as if she's the sweetest old woman in the world. "Anything you need, come and find me. I want your stay here to be a good one, despite what you've just heard."

As we follow her out, Jasmine rubs my arm in a show of solidarity, and I offer her a tremulous smile. That was a battle I wasn't expecting, and she could have probably saved her words because until I find Winter, I'm in no position to fall in love with anyone, even my gorgeous friend who has somehow been my guiding light through the madness.

Yes, there is something about Alessandro Majerio that is telling me that I have arrived in the middle of our story, and I wonder what the ending will bring.

CHAPTER 17

ALESSANDRO

We follow my grandfather outside and the usual buggy is waiting to take us the short distance to the headquarters. It's the building set some way from the house that he prefers to conduct his business in. A huge space constructed to look like a separate house, but inside the rooms are concrete and steel. The old Italian façade of a traditional building is a cunning disguise for what goes on inside.

As we exit the buggy, the cameras set up all around the perimeter follow our progress and as we enter through the huge oak studded door, I take in a breath of pure evil. Tormented souls, centuries old, scream at us to go back because one thing's certain in this crypt of the damned, you only get out if my grandfather says so.

Angelo is silent as we make our way down the dark, foreboding corridor to a steel door at the end, which is one of many that occupy this building. Offices, cells and the hospital, as my grandfather refers to his torture chamber, all make up a floor plan any realtor would run from screaming for salvation.

"Buona sera, Don Majerio."

The enforcer nods with respect and my grandfather says in his deep authoritarian voice, "Antonio, I trust our guest is waiting."

He nods and swings open the door, allowing us to pass through and I blink in disbelief when I see the unexpected frail body sitting in a wheelchair in the center of the dank, depressing room.

Strip lighting gives no indication of what time of day it is, and the polished marble floor is the best possible surface to clean the remnants of a person's body from life.

The walls are concrete and appear old and crumbling under the weight of the horrors it's witnessed through the years. However, the current resident of this halfway house to hell commands my attention because slumped in the chair and appearing as if he died already, is Massimo Delauren.

Once powerful Mafia Don feared and respected throughout the world is hovering between hell and damnation as he appears to be dead already.

"What's this?" I hiss and my grandfather shrugs, heading over to the wheelchair and jerking his thumb toward his guest.

"What's left of a tyrant, I'm guessing. Whatever your woman gave him did our job for us."

"What do you mean?" Angelo growls beside me because this is an anti-climax of the most frustrating kind.

A man steps forward who hovered close to the walls, wearing a white coat and carrying a clipboard of all things.

"Um, Doctor Giovanni, sir." He stutters, glancing between us all and my grandfather says pleasantly, "Luca, why don't you bring my grandson and our distinguished guest up to speed on the patient's progress?"

Clearing his throat, the doctor looks down at his clipboard more for reassurance, I'm guessing, because both Angelo's and my own anger are filling the space with rage and retribution.

"It appears the gentleman suffered a massive stroke. His

brain activity is normal, but his body is paralyzed. He has no control of it and is locked inside his own body with no hope of recovery."

"A stroke?" Angelo says in disbelief. "Can he hear us?"

The doctor nods.

"Yes."

"How do you know?" I growl, moving closer to peer into the eyes of the man I wanted to tear apart personally.

"His brain function is normal, and he reacts through expression in his eyes. He understands everything but has no way of communicating."

"Will he survive?"

I am keen to hear the answer to this because if he dies before I've made his life a living hell, I'll consider him lucky.

"He could live several years in this state. It's the worst kind of condition for the person affected this way. If the patient is left, they will die naturally, but if they are fed intravenously and monitored, they could live out the rest of their days for several years."

"So, Alessandro, Angelo."

My grandfather looks at us with interest. "The question is, what do you want to do about this interesting development?"

I glance at Angelo and his eyes mirror mine. The pain in them too raw to let Massimo dodge our particular brand of justice even though it appears he already has. He will never experience the pain of being tortured to death. Never discover what it's like to be cut apart, piece by piece. Whatever we do to him won't affect him at all and I never believed for one moment I would be faced with a decision like this.

Angelo stands before him and stares into Massimo's eyes and the dark stare he gives him makes my soul cower in fear.

"He will pay regardless." Angelo hisses and his lip curls in disgust as he addresses the man himself.

"You took something that belonged to us, and you broke

her. She is safe now and will heal and become the kind, loving, beautiful woman she is inside. You will not. You will suffer for as long as I say you will, knowing your own wife now lies in another man's bed."

I glance up in surprise as Angelo reveals the path this is going to take and just the pain in Massimo's eyes tells me his words have found their mark.

I step forward.

"Don Sontauro is right. Imogen is married to a Bratva Don and loves him with all her heart. She hated you, detested you, and couldn't wait to escape."

Only the madness in Massimo's heart is preventing him from seeing the facts. He truly believed Charlotte was his wife, despite having buried his own wife years ago. He imagines she lives and that will be his greatest pain picturing her with another man, just as I had to do when he took Winter from me. I understand the pain of that and the nightmares it brings, knowing there is nothing you can do about it.

Angelo curls his lip in disgust and delivers blow upon verbal blow.

"Her husband has taken your empire and together they command your army and run your businesses. They live in your home and enjoy the luxuries you paid for, knowing you will rot to death picturing their happiness. They laugh at you, and they have been laughing at you the entire time. How does it feel knowing they pity rather than fear you?"

We both lean forward and stare into his eyes, and I see the pain cutting him up from the inside out. It's obvious and yet we're not lifting a finger to touch him. It's interesting how much more effective the mind is as a weapon, especially when his was scrambled years ago.

"Just so you know, Massimo…"

I spit in his eyes. "I have my woman back by my side.

Winter is safe despite what you did to her, and you will never hurt her again. Oh, and if you think this is over, it's only just begun."

Angelo nods. "You don't deserve death. You deserve to be locked into your own mad brain and live with yourself for eternity. For now, we will leave you with your nightmares, knowing you are powerless against them. Say hi to your new home, Massimo, because you only get to leave when we've had our fun. Then we will pay for you to rot in hell inside an institution and pay them well to keep you alive for as long as possible."

My grandfather laughs but it has no humor in it and he comes and stands beside us, also peering into Massimo's eyes.

"It's interesting how men who think they are great are often confused by their own reflection. There are four of us in this room who command and determine people's fate. We believe we have that right. We do not. But we do it anyway. That's why we have no mercy, Massimo. You may consider we are brothers in arms, following the same path. You stumbled on yours years ago and somehow the evil in you manifested into madness. Some may say you put a dog down when it loses its mind. Those people are good people and we have just established we are not. Evil against evil, nobody will ever win, but in your case, we already have."

He turns to us and snarls, "Have your fun then move him out. He offends my eyes and just knowing he is here causes a cancer in my beautiful home. Only great men deserve great endings. He has proven he doesn't deserve that title."

With one last disgusted look, my grandfather turns and leaves the room and, as the door slams behind him, I say to the doctor. "Keep him alive."

As we turn away, I expect my heart to be lighter, relieved even, as if justice has been done. I'm not surprised to find I'm not even close to that. Massimo's last days on earth will turn into years because I have no humanity left inside me where it concerns him.

CHAPTER 18

WINTER

I am alone for the first time. Nonna showed me to a guest room and even though it's luxury on a grand scale, it scares me. Jasmine was shown to a different room and despite asking to stay with me, I could tell she was tired and so I pretended I wanted to be alone. I'm not.

Something is terrifying me. After hearing the harsh, brutal words of Alessandro's grandmother, I no longer feel welcome here. She is tolerating me because this is what her grandson wants, but even though we are just friends, she believes it could be something else.

He loves me. I replay the moment he said it over and over again and the fact it wraps around my heart and fills me with happiness makes me feel so guilty about that. I only know what they tell me and who knows if that's the truth. Until my memory returns, I can't make any decisions and as much as I want to fall into Alessandro's arms where I feel so safe, I know I have no right to be there.

Nonna was right. I am another man's wife. No longer a virgin and now don't qualify for the job of Alessandro's future one. I'm shocked that I'm disappointed about that. Why don't I want to find my husband? He's dead. Nonna's words tell me one thing, but it was obvious it isn't a physical state. Somewhere he is breathing and one day he will find me. I will be punished.

I shiver with fear because deep inside I'm waiting for it to happen, which means it's happened before. I am always being punished. Domestic abuse. That's what they told me and the fading bruises on my face and neck tell me they're right. Did he try to kill me? Or did somebody else? My world is a scary place right now, and something inside me is telling me it always was.

The darkness is oppressive despite the lamplight that illuminates the shadows in the room. The night sky is as black as my heart and as I stand by the window, there aren't any stars to shine and guide my way. I wonder where I go from here. Part of me wants to stay, the other wants to leave immediately.

But I don't want to leave Alessandro, despite what his grandmother says. He is my lifeline and without him, I am struggling under the waves of despair that are threatening to pull me under.

A soft knock on the door makes me jump and, wondering if Jasmine has come to find me. I say with a stutter, "Co… come in."

As the door opens, my heart flutters when the object of my thoughts fills the doorway, his eyes glittering in the darkness like a predatory beast sizing up his kill.

"Am I disturbing you?"

His husky tones make my heart leap and I say shyly, "No, please come in."

His body fills the room and I swallow hard because I can't tear my eyes away from him. There's something so commanding about Alessandro Majerio. From his wild shoulder length hair that has been tamed into a ponytail, the rough stubble on his face and the dark penetrating eyes usually covered by shade. He wears his black tailored suit paired with an partly buttoned black silk shirt, showing off a tanned and buffed torso that is scripted by dark tribal ink. His pants sit low on his hips and the leather shoes he wears must have cost a small fortune.

Yes, Alessandro is a magnificent man, and I can't ignore the power that surrounds him whenever he is near.

It's as if I'm so small in comparison, and he makes me shy and as he sits on the bed, he pats the space beside him.

"Come, we need to talk."

Like a docile servant, I do as he asks and am surprised when he reaches for my hand and laces our fingers together.

"I will say this again." His husky voice reaches out and settles my heart. "You are safe here and nothing will hurt you again all the time I am beside you."

"But how?"

"How what?"

"I can't stay here forever. You have a life, Alessandro, and I'm conscious I have steamed into it and blown it apart. You have a family; a job and I have…" I break off and sigh. "I have unanswered questions and a life that is hiding from me right now. I should just stay here until I remember, or then again, perhaps I should head back with my brother and Jasmine. They are my family, I guess."

For a moment there is silence and then he surprises me by saying, "What do you want?"

"Me?"

I'm a little shocked at that because, for some reason, it's as if nobody has ever asked me that.

I consider my answer and then say sadly, "I want my memory back."

"I see." He squeezes my hand and says with a sigh. "Be careful what you wish for, Winter. Some may say you've had a lucky escape, forgetting the past. Your future is what counts now and it can be anything you want it to be. You are young, in good health and have people who love you surrounding you. The world is yours for the taking and you just need to say the word and we will arrange it for you."

"We?"

"Me, your brother and your friends. We all want the best for you, and we always have."

"My friends." I roll the word around my mind and resist the urge to lay my head on his shoulder, because for some reason I am desperate to be close to him.

"Yes, do you remember when I spoke of Rockwell Academy?"

I nod and his voice softens. "There were seven of us living in a house. Angelo, me, Ivan, Flynn, Malik and Emma, your friend."

"I don't remember." I wish I did because it sounds as if I was happy there and he says gently, "You wanted your freedom, but Angelo made that impossible. He forced you to move in with us and insisted you brought your roommate to keep you company."

"Why would he do that?"

"Because he loves you and, well, your father had a different future for you mapped out."

"My father?" I am struggling to picture him and Alessandro snarls, "After graduation you were to be married to a man your father chose."

"My husband?"

He nods. "It turns out your father promised you to his friend Massimo Delauren and one night you never came home."

"What happened?" I'm so afraid for my past self and Alessandro growls, "We learned you were taken by a teacher to Massimo's house, where he married you and kept you prisoner. The only time we saw you was when the occasion dictated it and to the world, you appeared happy."

"Maybe I was."

Alessandro hisses, "You were far from happy. It was evident in your eyes and I'm guessing you were made to put on a show for our eyes only. What hold did he have over you, Winter? What did he threaten you with to make you do everything he asked?"

His words bounce around my mind like the draw for the lottery and yet none of them comes up with the answer I need.

"I don't remember." I place my head in my hands and whisper, "I hate this, Alessandro. There is something holding me back from seeing through the fog. It's as if it's so important to remember. I have nothing but anxiety and a fear of being punished, but I don't remember why."

I turn into his chest, allowing his strong arm to wrap around me as I struggle to remember. As his hand rubs low circles on my back, he says with a catch to his voice, "Would you like me to tell you how we became friends?"

I nod, just grateful for any bit of information he can give me, and he says in a softer voice, "When you came to Rockwell, Angelo warned us not to touch. You were under our protection because of the future waiting for you. You were to be a mafia bride and must remain untouched because if you went to your marital bed any less than a virgin, you wouldn't wake up the next morning."

I stiffen as Nonna's words come back to haunt me and Alessandro laughs softly, "You were so strong, Winter. So curious and so afraid that you would never discover what it was like to experience the passion of your first kiss."

"What are you telling me, Alessandro?"

I pull back and stare up into his dark eyes that are brimming with passion, and he tilts my head to face him and whispers, "You went there, anyway."

"With you?"

I hold my breath as he smiles. "One night only, that was

your request. Give you a memory to treasure in the dark days ahead."

The expression in his eyes and the emotions that swirl inside me are telling me he's speaking the truth. One night only sounds so familiar to me. Even a little of the fog clears in my mind as I let him inside and I'm discovering he has every right to be there.

"Show me." I whisper the words so quietly he raises his eyes. "What did you say?"

"I said show me what happened next."

I edge a little closer and, as his strong hand wraps around the back of my head, I lean in for something I want more than anything. His lips hover tantalizingly close to mine as he says, "Are you sure?"

"Kiss me, Alessandro. One night only you said. Why do I have the feeling that it was the best night of my life?"

As our lips touch, I close my eyes and my soul sighs with relief. His gentle pressure makes my heart ache as if he is frightened I will break. As I reach out and cup his face, I love the rough stubble against my fingers, and I lose myself in a kiss that's been a long time coming.

CHAPTER 19

ALESSANDRO

I couldn't stop now if I tried. Finally, Winter is in my arms where she belongs and despite everything, I believe we were always destined to find our way back to one another. Two years of torment after one night of passion tells me that night meant everything, to me, anyway. As I hold her in my arms, I feel so scared I will break her. I should be treading a careful path, but I can't resist the magnetic pull she has always held over me.

It's the sweetest sensation in the world kissing the woman I love and despite her fragility, I want this more than life itself and I always did.

Her soft moan against my lips makes my heart swell and as she holds my face in her gentle hands, I love every single fucking moment of this kiss. It's as if it's our first one and all the sweeter for the long wait we've suffered to arrive at this point.

There is no need to stop. I could kiss her all night and now we have started, there will be no stopping and as the minutes turn to hours, we just spend them in each other's arms.

As the night falls into dawn, we have spent every precious

minute touching, kissing and smiling into each other's eyes as we explore what this could be. I don't press any further because Winter needs to heal, and kissing is a step I never thought we would reach so soon after we came here.

The sun inches its fingers through the drapes and warns us it's time to rise and I must physically tear myself from my position beside her because we have business to attend to.

"Where are you going?"

She looks anxious and I smile reassuringly. "I should shower and change. Breakfast is at seven and be late at your peril."

She glances over at the clock by the bed and says with surprise, "We've been up all night."

"So it would seem." I chuckle and her eyes are wide as she whispers, "I'm sorry."

"For what?"

'For keeping you from sleeping. You must be exhausted."

"Are you?"

She wrinkles up her forehead and I want to kiss every line away. "No. I'm not."

"Then you have your answer."

I sigh and say with regret. "You should shower and change, too. Nonna has arranged a change of clothes and after breakfast..."

"What?" She looks anxious and I say gently, "You must spend time with Angelo. He leaves today and will be anxious to check on you."

"He's leaving me here?"

"Only if you're happy about that."

I am suddenly anxious because what if she wants to leave with them? I never considered that possibility for a second and now I'm not so sure.

"I want to stay with you." She appears shy as she speaks and the faint blush to her cheeks pulls me by her side in an instant.

Cupping that gorgeous face in my hands, I kiss her long and leisurely and make no secret of my intentions. When I pull back, the spark of desire I see in her eyes mirrors my own and I say roughly, "You are mine, Winter, and you were before you were snatched from my side. Don't feel guilty about this because you belong here."

"But how will this work?"

She seems sad all of a sudden, causing me to pull her against me to chase the shadows away.

She whispers, "I can't be with you, Alessandro."

"That's not what I want to hear, baby."

I growl and try to make light of it, but she pushes me away and says almost bitterly, "The first thing your grandmother told me was that you will inherit the title of Don Majerio."

"She is right." I'm a little surprised this is a problem, and Winter sighs and moves across to the window.

"You will need a mafia wife, not a divorced woman like me. Your grandmother told me that and said if I loved you, I would put you first and honor the traditions of a family that abides by them."

I can't believe I'm hearing this and say angrily, "Nonna said that."

"Don't be angry, Alessandro, she was only speaking fact. Jasmine herself had nothing to say because she ticked all the boxes herself. I am soiled goods; another man's cast off and I have no right to be your queen. Maybe we should stay as friends for all our sakes because I don't think I'm strong enough to fight this battle. Not now and it wouldn't be fair to you either."

"So, what are you saying?"

I almost can't speak, and she says firmly, "I just want to be your friend and if you can't accept that, I will leave with Angelo today. I'm sorry, it's for the best."

She turns away and I suppose my pride makes my decision

a bad one because, without another word, I storm out of her room and slam the door hard behind me. I will not allow her to make me weak. I will not beg and as for my grandmother, she had better have a very good explanation for this because now I'm pissed, and God help my family if they are backing away from their word now.

* * *

I WASTE no time and head straight for grandfather's den. I know he will be there. He always checks in with Salvatore before breakfast and I am not disappointed.

As I open the door without the courtesy of a knock, Salvatore steps in front of him and says questioningly, "Alessandro, I was unaware we had a meeting scheduled."

"Move aside, Salvatore." I growl and my grandfather's low laugh dispels the tension, and then his slow husky voice calls off his dog.

"Leave us, Salvatore. Alessandro obviously has something weighing heavily on his mind."

Salvatore fixes me with a hard look before moving silently away and as soon as the door closes behind him, my grandfather's eyes sparkle and he says roughly, "Sit, Alessandro, and explain this disrespect."

I take my usual seat and lean forward, staring him hard in the eye and snarl, "Nonna has overstepped the mark."

He leans back and shrugs. "In what way?"

"She warned Winter off and told her she had no place here. She was soiled goods and not fit to be a Don's wife."

"And you're surprised at that."

He shakes his head and smiles slyly. "She speaks the truth, and you know it. She has not overstepped the mark. She has highlighted it."

"But we had a deal."

The look in his eye would reduce a killer to train his gun on himself, but I stand my ground and face him off because I will not be treated as a fool.

"Alessandro. The deal we made was to liberate your friend. Job done, request fulfilled and now you must honor the agreement."

"Bullshit." I face him down and hiss, "You knew exactly what my interest in Winter was. At no point in the conversation did you inform me you expected me to marry somebody else."

"Did you ask?" He fires back. "I thought we raised you to understand our ways, Alessandro. A Don's wife must be a virgin on her wedding night. You would make this respected family a laughingstock and Nonna was right to bring it to your attention. Winter is Massimo Delauren's wife. That hasn't changed. The man locked in his own madness, who is a guest here of sorts. Winter Delauren is now her brother's concern, not yours. Do I make myself clear?"

As the truth hits home, I just stare at the wily old fox and realize I've been played. My grandfather agreed to help me to bring me to heel. He's right, there were no other guarantees than setting Winter free, but he's forgotten one important thing. I have his blood running through my veins and so I stand and lean over his desk, meeting him face to face and snarl, "Then understand one thing, Grandfather, or should I say Don Majerio."

He doesn't even blink and just looks at me with curiosity as I snarl, "If I can't marry Winter, then I won't marry. The Majerio bloodline stops with me, and your precious tradition will die with me." I stand up and throw him a curt nod.

"I'll see you at breakfast, Don Majerio."

I turn and walk away with fire in my heart. I have come too far to give Winter up without a fight and knowing my grandfather, this will be the fight of my life.

CHAPTER 20

WINTER

Breakfast was as awkward as fuck because the atmosphere was so tense, I could cut it with a swipe of my finger. Alessandro is brooding about something and won't even meet my eye or anyone's for that matter and apparently Angelo notices too, given the concern he throws in his direction.

Nonna is thoughtful and his grandfather silent and it's so wrong on every level and I'm grateful when it's over and Angelo says firmly, "Thank you for your hospitality, Don Majerio. Mrs. Majerio. If I may excuse Winter, I would like to spend some time with my sister."

I am so grateful for the excuse to leave and smiling my thanks, I follow my brother and Jasmine out of the room into the amazing, landscaped gardens.

Jasmine exhales sharply. "Whoa, that was tense. I wonder what happened?"

Angelo shakes his head. "God help Alessandro. He's delivered them his soul and I pity him that."

"What do you mean?" I'm curious and I don't miss the sharp stare Jasmine directs at him, causing him to sigh heavily.

"There's something you should know about Alessandro, Winter."

"Will I like it?" I'm concerned about that, and he shrugs. "That depends on how you feel about him."

"He's my friend."

Jasmine rubs my arm and whispers, "Is that what you feel in your heart?"

We carry on walking toward the huge sparkling lake, and I consider my feelings toward the brooding beast who lay beside me so tenderly last night.

"I don't know." I falter and wonder if I should say anything and, thinking better of it, I sigh instead.

"I should return home with you. Wherever that may be."

Angelo looks worried and a silent signal passes between them, causing me to say irritably, "Stop with the looks. What don't I know other than every fucking minute of my life until this point? Help me for God's sake, because I need you to fill in the gaps for me."

Jasmine whispers, "Tell her, Angelo, it's only fair."

Now I'm scared and he rolls his eyes and says irritably, "Ok, but things may have changed."

"What things?"

I am so confused and hating every minute of this, and Angelo takes my hand and pulls me down beside him on the grass, placing his arm around my shoulders and for some reason something stirs in my mind.

For a second he says nothing, and I give into the sensation we have done this before. Several times before and a faint memory of an orchard comes back to me of the perfect scene that is shattered by a piercing scream. I don't hear him speak because I am a child again. He is beside me and I am cold. So very cold, despite the warm sunshine stroking our souls with light fingers.

"Angelo." I whisper, and he stares at me with concern. "What?"

"I remember."

He turns to face me with an urgent stare and says quickly, "What do you remember?"

"We've done this before. It was always our thing."

"Yes, that's true. What else?"

"I feel so desperate. Somebody is screaming. It's death, isn't it?"

Jasmine stares in shock as Angelo snarls. "It was the day our father murdered our mother."

I nod, tears running down my face as I cast my mind back on the small child who learned the horror of what happens when a mafia wife reaches her use by date.

Jasmine whispers, "I'm so sorry, Winter."

I gaze up and smile as if it's of no consequence.

"I'm fine. Trust that the first memory to return is a bad one. Are there any good ones to follow, or should I stop trying now?"

I try to make light of the situation but I'm shaking inside, and Angelo says with a sigh. "There is one important memory I believe you need help with."

"Go on."

He resumes the position and this time I snuggle against him, loving how familiar this is. I have a memory and the sweetest part of all is that it's reminded me how much I love my twin.

"When Alessandro left Rockwell Academy, he didn't return here."

"Where did he go?"

"Hollywood. His grandfather agreed to help him on the condition that when he died, Alessandro would return to Sicily and take his place."

"What happened to change that?"

I'm curious and Angelo says gently. "He fell in love."

"He did."

"Yes. He fell in love with you, Winter, and when you were taken, it affected him in a way none of us saw coming."

I fall silent because he told me as much himself and Angelo says with sadness, "He couldn't let it rest. He was tortured picturing you with another. He threw himself into his work and was very successful. We had a plan to align ourselves with powerful families, to overthrow Massimo and bring you back to us. The best way to assure their loyalty was through marriage."

"You did what?" I'm stunned, and Jasmine nods beside me. "It's how I met your brother. He came to my father and agreed to marry me for his loyalty."

"No way." I stare at her in horror, and she laughs, throwing Angelo a loving gaze that settles my heart. "We fell in love, so without the plan, I wouldn't be as happy as I am now."

Angelo nods. "Things worked out for us, and Flynn was no exception."

"Flynn?"

Angelo nods. "He also played his part along with Ivan, but it was Alessandro who made the biggest sacrifice."

"What did he do?" I'm almost afraid to ask and Angelo says with a hint of bitterness in his voice, "He agreed to give up Hollywood and take up his position by his grandfather's side. Return to the family business on the condition his grandfather helped to set you free. You see, Don Majerio is the most respected mafia don in the world right now and his help would bring the other families into line. Massimo was the most feared and nobody would willingly go against him, so Alessandro started a mafia war just to bring you back to us."

"He did that for me?"

The tears spill when I see the enormity of what's been going on and it's almost too much to comprehend. Then Angelo says coolly, "You can't turn your back on him, Winter. Despite what you consider is right, your place is by his side. He offered to marry you at Rockwell Academy, so our father couldn't use you for his own advantage. He fell in love with you and if you leave with us, you are condemning him to his own prison in your place."

Angelo's words are harsh but find their mark and I contemplate what he's asking.

"So, you think I should stay and fight for us to be together?"

Angelo makes to speak, and I'm surprised when Jasmine interrupts him.

"It's not what we think, honey."

I smile at the fierce glare she directs at her husband.

"Ask yourself how you'd feel if you left him here? Would it matter to you? Can you imagine a life without him?"

"It's too early to tell." Angelo says angrily and I reply slowly, "It's not."

They stare at me in surprise, and I shrug. "I know in my heart I loved him once. It's so familiar whenever he is close. I'm safe with him and it's as if my life is complete with him, save for one nagging sensation that just won't go away."

"What?" Angelo says quickly and I shake my head. "I don't remember. It's as if something is missing and I shouldn't be here. Could it be my husband? Maybe it seems wrong because I am still married to him."

Angelo looks as if he is auditioning for Satan's job as he growls, "That man has no hold over you. He almost destroyed you, Winter, and now you are free. If you think something is holding you back, it's because he fucked with your mind. Let go of the past and accept it's better you remember nothing. You may sleep better at night. You have a new path to tread and this time the shoe is on the other foot because where Alessandro did whatever it took to set you free. It's your turn now. I'm not pretending this will be easy but understand one thing. My sister was fearless, strong and brave. She would never back away from helping another and if I know my friend, that is exactly why he fell in love with you."

As we sit looking across the lake, Angelo's words hit a nerve. I can tell he's speaking the truth and somewhere deep inside, I also realize I'm not going anywhere.

CHAPTER 21

ALESSANDRO

I need distance from my grandparents and fast. As soon as the others leave, I waste no time in pushing back from the table and heading straight for the gym. I realize I'm showing them disrespect, but they earned it. They know how I feel about Winter and now they're telling me I'm to marry a woman who has probably been chosen already.

As I pass through the mansion, I must be dragging the darkness behind me because the soldiers I meet look anywhere but at me and as I near the gym, I growl to the nearest one. "I need a sparring partner. You'll do."

He falters and I growl, "Now!"

He obviously knows better than to refuse and heads unhappily behind me as we head for the gym that is tagged onto the pool house. As soon as we step inside, I reach for the kit in my locker and note he does the same. We are encouraged to work out as much as possible to keep in fighting shape, and every soldier here spends a considerable amount of time in this very room. However, I spend more and am currently unbeaten in the ring. Only Ivan is my equal and I wish like fuck he was here now because I need to punch my way out of my bad mood before I head off to find Winter.

I owe her an apology for walking out on her and I'm guessing she's packing her bags right now to leave with Angelo and his wife later today.

As I step into the ring, bare chested and barefooted, I watch the soldier strap on his padding, which immediately tells me he's lost before we've even begun. It's as much about mental strength as physical and he has just informed me he's shit scared of being hurt.

Too fucking bad.

It takes five blows to knock him out cold and I almost growl with frustration. What was that? Pathetic. Another soldier heads through the door and immediately regrets it when I step over the body of one and snarl, "Take his place."

I don't even get the previous one medical attention because I'm too fired up to care. These men know the score and if they can't take the heat, they may as well be dead already.

This one is more skilled, and it takes ten blows to knock him out and sighing, I look at the two men groaning beneath my feet and my angry roar fills the space. The door clicks open, and I see my grandfather regarding me with a malevolent gleam in his eye and I snap, "Do you fancy your chances?"

He shrugs and approaches the ring, looking with disgust at the bodies still moaning on the floor and snaps, "Get the fuck out of here."

On hearing his voice, they crawl to the side and somehow manage to drag their sorry asses to the changing room and my grandfather says with anger lacing every word, "Pull yourself together, Alessandro, and don't be a child. You are a man, and we deal with our problems in a more calculating way."

"I'm open to suggestions."

I face him off, my chest heaving and the sweat dripping

down my body, my hair wild around my shoulders and the caveman inside me surfaces.

My grandfather throws me a towel and a bottle of water, and I catch them in each hand and he shakes his head as if disappointed with me.

"Do you think I wanted to marry Nonna?"

I take a swig of water and don't even bother to reply.

He moves closer and says roughly, "It was arranged by our fathers. A union to bring our families together into one powerful dynasty. I didn't understand at the time, but she was perfect for me. Strong, beautiful and astute. The perfect Don's wife."

I shrug and say nothing, and he sighs heavily. "At the time, I thought I was in love with a dancer. Grace Monroe was her name, and she intrigued me. I was besotted and needed to spend every waking minute I had with her and for the most part, I did. We were happy, I was happy, and I wanted to marry her. Then my father stepped in and bought her a one-way ticket to America. He told her if she stayed in Sicily, he couldn't guarantee her safety. He decided my fate for me."

"So you understand how that feels."

I stare at him with a dark expression, and he nods. "I know exactly how that feels and yet I knew my place. I married Nonna, and she made me extremely happy. She was everything my family wanted for me, and I couldn't fault her. We have enjoyed a long and happy marriage because we both accepted our place in it. She gave me three children, and it was unfortunate only one of them was a boy who grew up to be a big disappointment to me because, like you, he thought he had a choice."

"Is that what I am, a big disappointment?" I'm mildly curious, and he shrugs. "You could be. It depends on your decision now."

"My decision, grandfather, is final. I will only marry one

woman and if that's not to your liking, then I'll live in sin, as they say."

If I expected him to be angry, I'm surprised because he merely laughs out loud as if I cracked the most amusing joke.

"Have your fun, Alessandro, I understand you have some time to make up, but when the dust settles, you will see I am right. There is nothing stopping you from setting Winter up in an apartment nearby. Mistresses have more fun, anyway."

"Like Portia, nice tits, by the way."

The angry snarl on my grandfather's face tells me I've hit a nerve, and he hisses, "Now you go too far. When you have walked in my shoes, you have a right to comment. Until then, you will honor our agreement and do what the fuck I tell you to. You have three months from today. Enjoy your woman and make plans for the future, but they don't include making her your wife. Do I make myself clear?"

"Perfectly."

As he turns to leave, I say roughly, "Don't go saving for a wedding, grandfather. I meant what I said."

"Three months, Alessandro, and you will learn that I always win in the end."

As he leaves, I sink to my heels and place my head in my hands. Three months, he says. A lot can happen in that time and one thing he appears to have forgotten is that when he dies, I can make my own fucking rules and there will be nobody who can stop me from doing what the hell I want.

CHAPTER 22

WINTER

It's strange saying farewell to my brother and his wife after recently discovering them again.

As we stand in the courtyard, it hasn't escaped me that one important person is missing. Angelo tried to call him but his phone cut straight to voicemail and as their cars that are taking them to the airfield roll to a stop, I glance around me nervously because what if he's gone? What will I do then? Perhaps I should leave and recuperate with people who actually appear to care for me.

As the final bag is placed in the trunk, I observe Angelo shake Don Majerio's hand and thank him for everything. Jasmine steps forward and hugs me hard, whispering, "Call if it gets too much. Angelo will come and get you; you only have to say the word."

"Do you think Alessandro will come back?"

I whisper, and she nods, smiling through her anxious frown.

"Of course, he will come back."

As she says the words, she looks past me, and her expression relaxes as she smiles. "In fact, if I'm not mistaken, he already did."

As I turn, my heart goes into freefall when I see him step into the light of the courtyard, freshly showered with his hair slicked back and his black shades on. He looks strong and brooding, his tight t-shirt barely containing the rippling muscles that are struggling to be set free and the ink on his biceps make me weak at the knees.

My man, I know he is and as he comes to stand beside me, Jasmine moves away. He leans down and whispers huskily, "I'm sorry for walking out on you, baby. It won't happen again."

His fingers lace with mine and he tugs me gently to his side and as Angelo approaches us, he throws Alessandro a hard stare. "Are you good?"

"I'm good."

"And your problem?"

"What problem?"

I don't even begin to understand what they are talking about, but the tears well in my eyes when Angelo steps toward him and they hug it out as only the best of friends can do. The emotion is tangible and even Jasmine can't tear her eyes away and I hear Angelo whisper, "Look after my girl."

"I always will." Alessandro replies.

For some reason, I know I am meant to be standing here by Alessandro's side, watching my brother leave with his wife. It's as if this scene was always meant to happen and I'm not second guessing my decision at all. I wish I could shake the uneasiness I have that follows me around like an Angel on my shoulder, whispering that I will never be happy until I remember something important from my past.

Angelo leaves me until last and my tears fall as he takes me in his arms and buries his face in my hair. His hand wraps around the back of my head and pulls me in close, and I love how secure he makes me feel.

As he kisses the top of my head, he sighs heavily and whispers, "I hate leaving you for a second, but I have business that won't wait another day. I will always be here for you, Winter. I always have been, and you only have to say the word and I will come and get you, night or day. Whenever you need me, I will make it back to your side."

He pulls away and stares past me and I can almost touch the intensity of the exchange between the two friends even though I can't see it and Angelo says with a deep voice that means business, "Take care of her. I'm relying on you."

"You don't have to ask." Alessandro sounds emotional, which shows me how close they are.

With one last kiss, Angelo and Jasmine step into the middle car and, as the doors close, it immediately pulls away.

As the car disappears down the long driveway, it tears my heart in two and as Alessandro's hand finds mine, I register that we are now alone. The rest of the family has disappeared inside, and I wonder what happens next on this incredible journey.

He spins me around to face him and I almost step back at the emotion in his eyes as he pulls me against his chest and, leaning down, whispers, "Thank you."

"What for?"

"For staying."

"I couldn't leave." As I pull away, I stare up the magnificent beast before me and say shyly, "I may not remember loving you, Alessandro but I feel it."

I reach up and cup his cheek and love how he leans into it and his eyes close for the briefest second as I say softly,

"I love you, Alessandro. It's not a memory, it's part of my soul and imagining walking away from you caused me the greatest pain, and there was never any doubt that I would stay to fight for you."

"To fight?"

He looks confused, and I inject a little steel into my voice.

"Your family doesn't want me here, that's pretty obvious, but I believe you do and that's all that matters. They think I'm soiled goods, well who the fuck cares about that? I don't and I'm guessing neither do you. I will stand by your side and fight them all if it makes you happy because I owe you a lot more than my grateful thanks for rescuing me from something my heart tells me was wrong. Perhaps the memory will come back, and I'll see my past clearly, but I already belong with you, nobody else. So…"

I take a deep breath and lay my heart on the line and say with a smile, "I love you Alessandro Majerio and I will do everything I can to make things work between us. However you want that to be."

Before the last word even leaves my lips, he captures it in his and as his strong hand snakes around the back of my head and he grinds his lips to mine, it's as if I have traveled a long and weary road and I finally made it home.

CHAPTER 23

ALESSANDRO

It's like an explosion that sets fire to our past and allows us to step from the flames to meet the future. We bear the scars of that but ultimately have survived and as I kiss the woman I love, I can't stop. She is like a feast for a starving man and as I pull her body even closer, it just isn't enough.

I don't even care that we are being watched from every angle on every monitor in the property because Winter is in my arms where she should never have left.

It's only when the sound of tires crawling up the driveway alerts us, do we pull apart and I stare with surprise at the cavalcade of black cars that are sweeping to a stop.

Winter says fearfully, "Who are they? What's happening?"

"I don't know."

As I grip her hand tightly, I'm aware of a movement behind me and Salvatore, my grandfather's consigliere, steps into the sunlight and stands by my side.

"What's going on, Salvatore?"

"Don Giodano and his family have been invited to lunch."

"Don Giodano?"

I'm surprised because he heads up a rival family to ours and I wasn't aware they were friends now.

Salvatore says in a low voice, "Perhaps Mrs. Delauren would be more comfortable in her room until they have left."

Winter makes to pull away on hearing his words and I tighten my grip. "She stays with me."

Salvatore nods but I don't like the gleam in his eye and as the doors open and Don Giodano steps out, he says quickly, "You should welcome him in your grandfather's absence."

Knowing it would be disrespectful not to, I drop Winter's hand and step forward, my mood set to polite bastard.

"Don Giodano, welcome to our home."

He grips my hand in a bone-crushing handshake and his eyes slide from me to Winter and he nods respectfully. "Mrs. Delauren, please accept my condolences for your loss."

"My loss?" Winter looks confused, and the eagle-eyed Don takes it all in and smirks. "I see you have yet to be informed of your husband's ill health."

"For good reason." I fix him with a warning glare, and he nods, a small smile lying on his malevolent face.

I'm surprised when the door to the second car is opened and one of his soldiers helps Don Giodano's wife from the car. From the other side steps another woman and now I understand exactly what this is. An intervention of the most devastating kind.

I nod my welcome as they reach the Don's side.

"Mrs. Giodano and Allegra, may I welcome you to our home."

The smile Allegra flashes me is seductive and loaded with intent. She bats her long lashes in my direction and appears shy, but she is anything but. She is a conniving bitch who is intent on securing the best possible marriage and as her dark green eyes sweep over Winter with derision, I feel the prison gates slamming shut in my face.

"Mrs. Delauren, such a terrible tragedy. Poor Massimo, you must be out of your mind with worry."

Beatrice the Don's wife vomits insincerity and heads straight to Winter's side and takes her arm.

"We should stick together being two wives of very powerful men. Even though yours is, shall we say, incapacitated, you are still to be given the respect you deserve."

Salvatore nods respectfully and says, "Follow me. Don Majerio is waiting for you on the terrace."

As they sweep past me, it leaves Allegra to step by my side, and she smiles seductively and says in a flirtatious voice, "Alone at last, Alessandro."

"Then we should join the others."

As I make to leave, she places her hand on my arm and whispers, "Wait, there's something you should know before we go inside."

"I'm listening." I move away so her arm falls to her side, and she says with a hint of victory in her expression, "This visit was arranged between your grandfather and my father. An alliance of sorts, shall we say. A lowering of weapons and a ceasefire so the treaty can be drawn up."

"What are you talking about? Just say what you're itching to get off your chest."

She steps closer and I can almost taste her breath as she whispers, "We are to marry to unite our families. If you refuse, it will start a bloody war because my family will view it as a great sign of disrespect. This is our engagement party, Alessandro, and by the end of it, we will be committed to merging a dynasty."

"Like fuck it is." I growl and she rests her hand on my arm and says with a soft sigh. "Just think about it. We would make a formidable couple. Two powerful families becoming one. I would be the wife you deserve and will bear your children. We will be good together. Just give us this chance."

I tear my arm away and growl, "I'm not interested in starting a dynasty with you. I have told my grandfather of my wishes and he had no right to plot behind my back. You may as well step back inside the car and leave because there will be no engagement today."

"Because of her, I suppose."

Allegra almost spits the words out and I freeze, before saying icily, "She has a name and it's Winter."

"Yes, Delauren. A married woman whose husband is still alive. She is no wife for you Alessandro, but I am. If you want to play with her from time to time, I won't like it but will accept that's your right, but I will bear the name Mrs. Majerio, not her, so grow up and be the man your grandfather thinks you are before I change my mind."

She takes my arm and hisses, "If I were you, I'd play along because my father is not the accepting kind."

I feel ambushed. Just when I thought I had it all worked out, another blow is dealt that leaves me staggering to get up.

As we walk into the lion's den, I know better than to cause a scene, Allegra's right about that and as we head onto the terrace, I immediately search for Winter who is perched unhappily between Nonna and Beatrice and from the expression on her face, she's burning in hell alongside me.

* * *

Typically, the only seats available are at the opposite end of the table and I reluctantly sit beside Allegra, noting the unhappiness in Winter's eyes. Grasping the decanter of wine, I fill our glasses and raise mine to my grandfather before knocking it back like water.

The glint in his eye warns me to behave and as Allegra leans closer, the stench of her perfume makes me want to hurl.

"Alessandro, tell me about yourself."

She purrs up at me, resting a proprietary hand on my arm, and I don't miss the smug look she sends down the table to the only woman I want touching me.

"Business. It's always business."

Her false laugh grates on my nerves as she shakes her head. "I would have expected no less."

As the food is delivered in abundance, I can tell my grandfather is pulling out the big guns and know it must be important to him to forge this alliance. Nonna throws me a warning glare every so often and as the conversation flows so does the wine.

Winter is playing her part well, but I can tell it's putting a strain on her and right now I detest my family. As Don Giodano watches my interaction with his daughter, I try so hard to contain the situation before it spirals out of control.

The moment comes sooner than I think when Don Giodano transfers his attention to us and says loudly, "I believe you have an announcement to make, Alessandro."

The fact his daughter's hand is stroking my arm makes it appear we are a lot closer than we are and I don't miss the triumph in my grandfather's eyes as he laughs softly. "To be young and in love again, Vittorio. I remember what that was like."

The stricken expression on Winter's face is all I need to shake off Allegra's unwelcome attention and say bluntly, "Yes. To answer your question, Don Giodano, I do have an announcement to make."

The angry glare from my grandparents warns me from speaking out of turn and the way Winter is looking down into her glass tells me she fears the worst.

"I'm leaving."

Startled eyes glance in my direction and the anger on my grandfather's face is palpable.

He knows better than to interrupt and Don Giodano glares at him angrily. "Leaving! Where?"

His wife shares a look with Allegra, who pouts like a petulant child, and I say firmly, "My grandfather has agreed a sabbatical for three months while I put my affairs in order."

I glare at him pointedly and note the resignation in his eyes. He can't back away from his own words and I take great pleasure in looking directly at Winter and smiling softly. "Yes, our flight leaves in the morning."

"Our flight?" Allegra looks at me sharply and I nod, dismissing her with a bored expression.

"Mrs. Delauren will accompany me to Canada. We have unfinished business to attend to, and I will be gone for three months."

Nonna raises her eyes to the heavens and looks despairingly at her husband, who just nods as if this was his plan all along.

"It is true." He concedes to the furious Don beside him. "Alessandro has three months to finish what he started and then return to take up his position by my side. He will be ready to accept what that involves. Isn't that right, my boy?"

His stern warning is noted, and I nod. "Three months, grandfather, as agreed."

I pointedly ignore his question and, taking that as my cue to leave, I stand and toss my napkin on the table before saying to Winter, "Mrs. Delauren, I believe we were about to make the necessary arrangements. If you will excuse us, we really should be getting back to business."

Turning to Allegra, I nod politely and relish the rage clouding her narrowed eyes before I turn to our guests and nod with respect and then walk from the terrace with Winter hot on my heels.

CHAPTER 24

WINTER

I almost have to run to catch up with him, and as Alessandro strides as far away from the terrace as he can, I cast my mind back on an extremely uncomfortable meal. It was as if I was a cuckoo in the nest and I detested every minute of it. I understood immediately what Alessandro's grandparents were doing, and I hated them for it.

As we turn the corner, I'm surprised when Alessandro pushes me roughly against the wall and wastes no time in kissing me like a man on his way to the gallows. I'm guessing he feels that way and so I return the kiss with every ounce of emotion I have.

The passion is raging between us, and it's taken me by surprise a little. Why do I crave him so much? It's as if this kiss is a long time coming and I'm convinced if we were alone in a bedroom, we would both be naked by now. It's as if he possesses every fiber in my body and fills my heart with his image, scent, and mind. Alessandro Majerio owns me, and I think he always has.

He breaks away and my lips feel fuller, swollen even, and yet the taste of him on them is the sweetest one in the world. I am so happy, and I'm surprised when he growls, "It's time to end this shit."

"What do you mean?"

I'm a little worried about that and he sighs heavily.

"I always believed the hardest part would be to bring you back to me. Unharmed and willing to pick up where we left off."

"But that happened. I'm here and I want this. I want you."

He strokes my face lightly and stares deep into my eyes and whispers huskily, "I want the whole of you, baby. I want the woman I fell in love with, and I want the innocent girl who dreamed of love. I want to give that to you, but there is something standing in our way."

"What?" I'm almost fearful of his answer and he growls, "Your husband."

"But he can't hurt me now. You told me he is as good as dead."

He touches my lips lightly with his and it calms me in a heartbeat and then he whispers, "He may be able to help us."

"I don't understand."

He pulls me close and kisses my forehead lightly. "You have lost your memory. It's hurting you; I can tell that."

I nod, a lone tear splashing onto his fingers as my voice breaks. "I only know what you tell me. I have feelings that are guiding me, but there is something I'm missing that's making me on edge. It's as if I need to see the whole picture to be truly happy again. I have a great fear of being punished and I'm worried about that. Is there someone coming for me I have forgotten about? Was it really my husband, or somebody else? I kind of think there is another person involved in my story, and I'm scared, Alessandro."

"Do you trust me, baby?"

He strokes my face so tenderly my lip trembles as I nod. "Of course."

"Then I have someone I would like you to meet. The person who may just light the spark that brings your memory back."

"Who?"

"Your husband."

I stare at him in shock, and he looks so angry I wonder if this was a good idea. Suddenly, I'm afraid—really afraid. It's as if a huge bolder is heading down a mountain toward us, increasing in strength, ready to crush us to death.

I'm having a panic attack, I must be and only Alessandro's calm words keep me from screaming.

"I've got you, baby. He can't hurt you now, but he may be the key that will unlock your mind."

"I don't think…" I'm struggling to breathe as an unknown force presses down, trapping the air inside my lungs. I'm drowning in fear and yet Alessandro holds me close and provides comfort as only he can, and I understand this is a meeting that needs to happen.

I take a deep breath and say tentatively, "Ok."

"You agree."

He sounds proud and I stare up at him in surprise.

"There she is." He strokes my face lightly and I shiver with need as he says gruffly, "The girl who always stood up for herself. She didn't back down and took no shit. You are the bravest woman I have ever met, and that bravery will get you through this."

"I disagree." My voice shakes as I say wretchedly, "I am weak. I may have been brave once, but that's been torn away from me, leaving only the jagged edges. I'm only prepared to face him with you beside me. That doesn't make me brave, Alessandro."

"Bullshit, baby." He winks, which makes me smile.

"Winter Sontauro is a fighter and that fight back begins now. We both have our battles, and we will face them together."

He twists my fingers in his and raises them to his lips,

staring deep into my eyes the entire time, giving me the strength to get through this, and with a hardening resolve, I nod.

"Then let's go."

* * *

We walk silently, side by side, and I'm surprised when he stops by a buggy and helps me inside.

"It's not far, but too far to walk in the heat of the sun." He smiles his encouragement, and I try desperately to calm my frantic heart.

As we set off away from the main house, something about this seems familiar. It's almost as I was brought up knowing places like this existed. I'm guessing my own childhood home was much the same as the memory of what happened near to the orchard that day comes back to haunt me.

I sigh and Alessandro says quickly, "What?"

"I'm just wondering if all my memories are bad ones."

He shakes his head and says with a wink. "Not all of them, I hope."

My face is on fire because I'm guessing we shared more than just one kiss back at Rockwell and I'm even more surprised to discover that I want to make new ones, today if possible.

The cart stops at a building that on the outside looks like a smaller version of the mansion we came from. However, as soon as we step inside, I can tell this is no home. It's purely business in every way.

Alessandro nods to the guard on duty who peers at us with a curious expression and as I follow him down the dark corridor, my heart starts thumping with fear. What will I find? Will my husband be beaten, in pain, unrecognizable? Will he be angry with me? Does he have any power here? We stop outside a steel door and Alessandro places his hands on my shoulders and looks worried.

"If it's too much, we'll walk away. Angelo made me promise not to bring you here, but well, I'm doing it for all the right reasons."

"I know that." I take a deep breath. "I want to remember. I need to remember and if this helps that happen, I would be a fool not to try."

Dropping a light kiss on my lips, he rests his head against mine and whispers, "Then prepare to conquer your demons, baby."

The door opens and we head inside, and I blink at the sterile space that's a little familiar somehow. I'm guessing it's because of the hospital, which is exactly what this appears to be.

White marbled floors are clean and there is a strong scent of antiseptic in the air, but I'm more surprised to see the wheelchair placed in the center of the room where a slumped figure lies.

"Is that him?" I whisper, holding onto Alessandro's hand so tightly it must hurt, and he nods.

"Massimo Delauren. Once powerful Mafia Don brought to his knees and locked in a living hell."

"What happened?" I blink in surprise and Alessandro laughs softly and pulls me closer.

The man doesn't even move, as Alessandro says loudly, "We set up a meeting in a restaurant to rescue you. We had planned it down to the very last detail. My grandfather had paid all of Massimo's men off and they had agreed to switch their loyalty to him."

He laughs out loud. "Not that Massimo knew, of course. He thought he had the upper hand as always and believed we were walking into an ambush. But we were never going to take a chance with you. Whatever happened that day, you were coming back with us, and Massimo would leave Scarpetta in a body bag. I was hidden from his view with my gun trained on his head and as soon as the diversion arrived, I was to take him out."

He laughs and circles the body of a living corpse and shakes his head. "Then everything changed. Just before I pulled the trigger, you stepped into the line of fire. Before anyone registered what was happening, you injected him with something that obviously terrified the shit out of him."

"It was me?" My eyes are wide as I look at the man I brought to his knees and Alessandro nods. "He fell and took you down with him, which is why you hit you head. So, it was you who brought the great Massimo Delauren down and I'm guessing it was an act of desperation to set you free from a mad man."

I inch a little closer and stare at the man who appears so defenseless now. "But he's so old." I curl my lip in disgust and Alessandro spits, "You can thank your father for that. He promised you to his friend, and you never got a say in the matter. He kept you locked in his mansion and made you his wife before we even knew you had gone."

I stare at the man in front of me and watch a flicker of emotion spark in his eye, telling me he recognizes me. I stare a little closer, looking for a sign that I remember anything about him at all, but all I feel is revulsion that this man called himself my husband.

The more I stare, the braver I am, and something stirs deep inside that is growing.

Alessandro stands beside me and takes my hand and I whisper, "You say I'm this man's wife."

"I'm afraid so baby, but Angelo is arranging the divorce as we speak."

"I don't need a divorce, Alessandro."

His hand tightens on mine, and he says gruffly, "What do you mean?"

I peer into the crazed eyes of a stranger and one thing is as definite as I'm standing here. One memory is returning and far from being a bad one, it's one that fills my heart with relief.

Turning to Alessandro, I say with determination.

"I don't need a divorce because we never married in the first place and I can state as fact that I have never had sex with this man in my life."

CHAPTER 25

ALESSANDRO

I never expected that. I stare at Winter in shock, and she nods, a determined glint in her eye. "This man may still be a stranger to me, hovering like a shadow out of focus in my mind, but I see the day as clearly as we are standing here."

"Tell me." My heart is pounding because this is big news, to me, anyway, and Winter laughs with relief.

"The day I was taken, I remember something. A conversation that I'm hearing now. The details may be blurred, but the words are not. He told me that I was to be his wife and I strongly disagreed. I told him I would never marry him. He would have to kill me first. He didn't seem to care and just told me that to the outside world, we would be husband and wife. Nobody would question him and there would be no need to go through the formalities. He would arrange the paperwork and the actual ceremony wouldn't be required. I remember being so afraid of what that would mean, and I can hear him laughing as he told me he wasn't interested in me for sex. He preferred boys, anyway, and I would be just a figurehead, a wife in word only, an adornment on his arm and a smokescreen to fool the outside world."

She shakes her head and smiles so happily it's infectious and the relief we share at this news is like a cluster bomb of emotion exploding in my face.

"I'm not married, Alessandro. This man is not my husband."

She stares at me with so much delight in her eyes I can't resist reaching for her and pulling her close, kissing her so deeply her groan sets my libido on fire. Not that it changes how I feel about her, but it's like a refreshing shower over my soul. Winter is not married, which changes everything.

We almost forget we have a silent audience and as I kiss her deeply, I am consumed by passion. I have waited so long to have her in my arms, I could spend hours kissing her without coming up for air. She is my breath, she is my beating heart, and she is the blood that fills my veins. Winter is everything to me, and her past is now a dark memory that I will not allow her to drag into our future.

She pulls back and the sparkle in her eye matches my own and she whispers, "I can't wait another minute, Alessandro."

I know exactly what she means and with a huge grin, I take her hand and turn to face the shell of the man who once wielded so much power, driven through fear.

"Our business here is done."

I make to pull away, loving the madness dancing in Massimo's eyes, almost hammering to get out as he is locked inside his own worst nightmare.

"Wait." Winter stops and pulls me back.

I look at her in surprise and she says anxiously, "What are you going to do with him?"

"It's not my decision. I'm guessing your brother will have the final say, but we need to talk though the best plan."

"Don't kill him." She sounds adamant about that, and I wonder why.

Then she turns to face him and hisses, "I may not remember what he did to me, but I know the horror of it. Death will be too good for him. Too easy. He needs to suffer for a long time because of what he did. Promise me you will keep him alive and that it will be a living hell."

The fire in her eyes and the anger in her voice cause my own heart to lurch with a sudden burst of longing. There she is. My woman. The one I fell in love with and the reason I have been to hell and back. One night will turn to many more and my grandfather can go and fuck himself if he thinks I will marry anyone other than this amazing woman whose bravery makes me bow down before her.

As I reach for her hand, I have only one destination in mind and don't want to waste another second here in this crypt of the damned.

* * *

WE HEAD OUTSIDE, leaving Massimo with his own mad brain for company and as we head back to the house, I note the cars are still out the front. We take the rear entrance instead and I grip Winter's hand with determination and waste no time in heading to my bedroom on the top floor.

She almost has to run to keep up with me and as I push her inside, I slam the door behind us and turn the lock, loving how she faces me, her chest heaving, and her eyes lit with desire.

With no words, I tear off my shirt and step out of my pants, loving the way her eyes dilate and she runs her tongue around her lips, causing them to shine like a beacon. As she takes my lead, she shrugs out of the dress Nonna provided her with and I much prefer the bare-chested version as she stands in all her naked beauty. It's a view I have visited many times in my memory, but now I have no need for them because Winter is here in the glorious flesh, and I drop to my knees to worship the goddess I have craved for so long.

I waste no time in pressing my mouth against her soft pussy and with one swipe of my tongue, I relish fucking paradise. Months and years of denial make this all the sweeter because there has never been another woman since her. Many wouldn't believe that, but I have stayed true to her. The opportunities were limitless, but I tossed their advances aside and held onto the memory of the only woman I ever wanted in my arms.

As I take my reward for my patience, her gasp of pleasure fills my heart and as I taste sweet nirvana, my balls tighten in anticipation.

She fists my hair and pulls it free from the binding and as it sifts through her fingers, I dine on the most delicious meal. Her soft sweet juices coat my mouth and I feast as if it's my last meal on earth. She shivers as she stands naked before me and as her body shudders and releases on my tongue, her small gasp of pleasure is the sweetest sound in the world.

Stepping up, I pull her close until her tits are flat against my chest and devour her pretty little mouth so hard it must hurt. Her fingers claw through my hair sending me into a lust-filled frenzy and her nails scratching my back reveals the beast has met his mate.

With a low growl, I push her back on the bed and force her legs apart, roughly and without care, so I can feast my eyes on the treasure I've waited so long to find.

Her glistening pussy tells me she's so ready for me now and I almost don't want to spoil this perfect moment. I waste no time in reaching for a condom and I tear the packet with my teeth and with one sharp move, sheath my cock. Her eyes are wide as she stares at my throbbing weapon and yet there is no fear, just desire that lights up her face.

Dropping between her thighs, I push two fingers inside and

rub the edge of her throbbing clit and she arches her back from the bed with a low moan of impatience.

"Do you want me, baby?"

"More than anything." She sounds also desperate, irritable even, and I laugh softly as the crown of my cock nudges against her entrance.

I almost can't see straight as I grab one of her legs and hold it over my arm, just to deepen the moment when I take up ownership once more. Knowing the last man who entered this paradise was me, fills me with a hunger that I'm glad she can't see right now because I am one possessive bastard over this woman and fuck anyone who tries to take her from me.

She pants with desire, her eyes fixed on mine as we both anticipate a moment neither of us really expected would happen. With a hiss of desire, I inch slowly inside, careful not to tear the soft flesh that has guarded this treasure for so long. As I slide inside, her wet heat sets me on fire and her small moans of pleasure increase the deeper I move.

"Alessandro, oh my God, that's so good."

Her frenzied cry lights the spark that drives me and as I thrust fully inside, it's the greatest pleasure in the world.

"Baby, I've missed you so much." I growl against her throat as I bite it gently, licking and sucking, desperate to mark this woman as mine. Warning others to stay away because she is protected. She is mine.

I lift her leg higher and push in deeper and as my rhythm increases, she claws at the silk sheets like a wild animal. "Oh my God, you are so good." She gasps against my chest and as our sweat joins into one immense river, it glides between us, allowing the rhythm to increase.

Her tits are squashed against the ink on my chest and her tight pussy is stretched around my cock, squeezing it, owning it and promising it a happily ever after because she is going nowhere.

With every thrust, every moan, and every kiss, I make a promise to love her forever. As she calls out my name, I hope it floats on the breeze toward the diners outside, so they know who they're dealing with.

The moment I sense her orgasm build, my own rushes to meet it and I couldn't hold back if I tried and as I roar and she screams, life couldn't be more perfect than this moment when we explode with a mixture of relief, passion and love.

CHAPTER 26

WINTER

I'm in heaven. Pure fucking heaven and, as I lie crushed by the weight of the beast, I wouldn't want it any other way. I can feel his heart pounding against mine and I don't know where I end, and he begins. Finally, I have what I've waited so long to experience again. One night only was what we had, but the memory doesn't live up to the reality. So many emotions played a part in this, and I still can't quite comprehend we reached this point.

I press light kisses across his chest, and he drags my face to his to take his fill. His tongue wraps around mine and I taste my own desire on his breath and words are not required, as our bodies do the talking for us.

Despite still being inside me, I sense his cock hardening and blink in disbelief as he swells inside my tight pussy. He bites my lower lip, causing my stomach to flutter and as he drags his finger through my own orgasm; he pushes it inside my mouth which I suck, loving how erotic this is. Then his dark eyes flash as he holds my wrists above my head and growls, "Now for the main course."

My body comes alive as he rocks gently inside me, the

earlier frantic moves a sweet memory. This time Alessandro makes love to me. With care, gentleness, and love in his heart. Gentle touches replace rough ones. Soft kisses caress the storm of before. Light fingers trace a path across my heart and whispered words of love bind me to him forever. This is love at its most powerful. Two people together at last pledging their souls for eternity and forging a path through the barriers with one common aim. Love.

The second orgasm is just as sweet as the first. Softer, longer and like a leisurely end to the perfect day. This time we float back to earth on a cloud of love, not lust, and I wouldn't be able to say which one I prefer. As long as it's with him, it's all good and despite the circumstances that brought me here, I wouldn't change a thing. I belong in this position, and he belongs with me. There was always something so compelling about Alessandro Majerio and I doubt that will ever change.

Day turns to night, and we remain as close as two people can be. In the moments when we aren't exploring each other's bodies, we explore our minds instead. So much to catch up on and so much to say, and I am greedy for every detail of what happened since we were all together last. As he talks of the special time at Rockwell, the memories gradually return. While he speaks, I remember, and it becomes an exciting game. Somehow my memory is returning, albeit slowly and only when prompted by happy memories of the past. I love listening to him talk with his husky voice, the Italian accent caressing his words. He can't seem to bear it if one part of his body isn't touching mine and I'm the same.

Our need for food makes us reluctantly shower and dress, and I'm a little worried about the reception we may get. I'm guessing the guests have long departed and as I take Alessandro's hand, I wonder where the next metaphorical blow will come from.

We head into a kitchen that is silent and empty and I

breathe a sigh of relief as Alessandro heads to the cupboard and starts pulling out ingredients.

"What are you doing?"

I'm surprised to find he appears to know his way around the kitchen, and he grins. "Pasta, of course."

"I didn't know you could cook."

"I'm Italian, baby, of course I can cook."

He drops me a wink, making me giggle, and as he begins to prepare the food, I make my way to his side.

"Can I help?"

He raises his eyes. "I don't know, can you?"

"With direction—possibly."

He nods and tucks a stray strand of hair behind my ear and whispers, "First you can pour us some wine, then you chop tomatoes. Lots of tomatoes."

He winks and turns back to his job in hand, and I'm light spirited as I search for two glasses and a bottle of red.

It's so good to be doing something normal for once. I'm struggling to remember anything at all, but I'm guessing cooking isn't one of my skills if I'm honest. We were brought up with chef's, maids and people who carried out the domestic chores and I expect it was the same and still is for him However, Alessandro is obviously a master chef because the air is soon filled with the aroma of bacon, onions and lots and lots of tomatoes.

It doesn't take long, and we are soon sitting hunched together on the terrace outside, spoon feeding one another penne pasta and loving every minute of it. We talk in between mouthfuls of anything and everything just to make this magical night last as long as possible and I love the happiness that gleams in his eyes as he stares into mine.

The bottle of wine is soon empty and as my eyes start to drop, Alessandro wraps his arms around me, my head resting on his shoulder as we gaze up at the stars.

He whispers, "I used to look at these stars and wonder if you were watching them too."

"You did?"

I'm a little shocked at that because this man doesn't seem the type for sentiment.

"I hoped you were thinking about me as much as I was you. I tried not to imagine you with him."

"I'm not surprised." I make light of it, but a shiver passes through me when I think about the wasted shell of a human being not far away and I say sadly, "Part of me never wants to remember the past two years but there's a huge part of me that's telling me I must."

"Why?"

"Closure perhaps."

I sigh and stare up at the brightest star, and once again it's as if an important part is missing. It surprises me because it appears that life has worked out just fine in the end, but something deep inside me is telling me there is something essential I need from my past.

Alessandro also appears preoccupied, and I don't want to ruin this perfect day by dragging up the past, but I need to concentrate on healing my mind because until that happens, I can never truly be happy.

* * *

MORNING DAWNS with the promise of a fresh start. Before I even open my eyes, the warmth spreads through my body as it remembers the night of its life. I don't believe there's any part of it that Alessandro didn't focus his attention on at some point last night, and the delicious ache of satisfaction makes me stretch and moan with contentment.

As I reach for him, I'm disappointed to find the space next to me empty and as I turn, I can sense immediately I'm alone.

Rubbing my eyes, I sit up and wince as the soreness between my legs tells me we went a little too far yesterday, but I still wouldn't change a thing. I loved every minute of it and part of me wishes that day could have lasted forever.

As I drag my body from the bed, I wonder what today will bring. Alessandro said we were leaving, and I wonder where we're heading. As I shower, I lean back against the marble tiles and love how free I am because something is telling me freedom wasn't something I enjoyed until now. It's an alien feeling that I'm adjusting to, and my memory may be battered and crawling back to me inch by inch, but it's the future that interests me now.

I just hope Alessandro's grandparents allow us to have one.

CHAPTER 27

ALESSANDRO

My grandfather is pissed. It's obvious from the hard gleam in his eye and the frown on his face. He is sitting on the terrace nursing an espresso and as I stretch my legs, I lean back in my seat and contemplate him through hooded eyes.

It's just the two of us and I have filled him in on what Winter told me yesterday. If I thought, it would change his mind though I was wrong because he merely looks irritated before sighing heavily.

"This changes nothing."

"It changes *everything*."

"It changes nothing." He repeats the sentence with a low growl.

"The alliance has been arranged and if we pull out now, there will be blood. Are you prepared to sacrifice your soldiers, possibly your own life, for a woman?"

"I would sacrifice everything for Winter. I already have."

I remind him why I'm here at all and then lean forward and say firmly. "You knew I gave my freedom up for her. Did you really believe I'd watch her walk away from me?"

He rolls his eyes and spits, "I'm not asking you to give her up. Just enjoy a different kind of relationship. Allegra knows how this works. She will turn a blind eye to your activities outside the home, but she will demand your respect in it. Nonna was the same and I'm guessing Beatrice suffers along with the rest of them. Our role comes with many perks to ease the burden of the day. You can have it all, Alessandro and I'm disappointed that you are blinded by love."

He leans forward and fixes me with a stern expression. "Love has no place in our world. Lust has free reign, and duty wins every time. Take your three months and when you return, it's attending your own wedding and your bride will be waiting for you with the greatest gift a man like you can have. Power. It's all about power, Alessandro and Winter Delauren has none."

"It's Sontauro." I hiss through bared teeth.

"She has never, or ever will be, a Delauren. You say I would rather sacrifice my own soldiers than give her up. I disagree. You understand how this works, Grandfather; you scripted the rulebook. You say I would be weak if I backed away from this union. I disagree. True weakness is doing what's expected. What the enemy wants you to do. Power comes from making a stand and winning through planning and manipulation. I always thought you were a master at that, and I hope you don't prove me wrong."

For a second we stare at each other through identical malevolent eyes and then I stand, my voice reaching across the table with a thousand blades attached. "I'll be gone for three months, grandfather and when I return, the only bride by my side will be Winter. There will never be a vacancy in that position for anyone else. If you want a weak man to stand in your shoes, you chose the wrong one in me. Perhaps you should give my father another try. He may be scared enough of you to agree."

As I turn, his voice jumps out and grabs me by the throat with a dark warning. "Don't challenge me, boy. Duty manifests itself in many ways and claims the souls of the strongest men. This is bigger than either of us, and I will do whatever it takes for the good of the family. That is what matters more than anything. The Majerio family and if you want to be included in that, you will play your part or be damned."

"Are you seriously threatening me?"

I turn slowly and stare at him with anger flashing in my eyes and I'm surprised when he stands and moves toward me, facing me with the eyes of a grandfather this time and not my Don.

As he reaches out and pulls me in for a hug, he whispers, "Three months, my boy. If you can find a way to have it all, I will be the proudest grandfather in the world. If your decision costs lives, it may just be yours that's sacrificed."

I pull away and nod, noting his battle lines. Three months to work a way out of this madness and return to honor our agreement. Luckily for me, I have powerful friends who will enjoy every minute of the challenge set and I can't wait to get back behind friendly lines because I may have won the battle in freeing Winter, but the war is far from over.

* * *

Things move fast and we are soon taking our seats on my grandfather's private jet and heading for Canada.

Winter is quiet beside me and as the wheels leave the ground, I'm conscious she is worrying about something.

As the plane levels off, I reach for her hand and lace our fingers together and she smiles with a hint of nerves.

"Where are we going?"

"Club Mafia."

She nods and I wonder why she asked because I told her

that when I instructed her to pack what she had because we were leaving.

It worries me because she is forgetting things; new things, not memories, and I wonder if she needs further medical attention.

Turning to face her, I stare at her with concern, and she shrugs. "What?"

"I told you where we were going. Had you already forgotten that?"

"No, I remembered the name, but you never told me what it is."

Now I feel like a fool and exhale, lifting her hand to mine as I kiss every finger. I don't think I will ever stop craving this woman and every minute I'm not touching her is a wasted one.

The attendant brings us a glass of champagne and as soon as she leaves, I raise my glass to Winter.

"To our future, baby. I intend on it being a long one."

She smiles, but I hate seeing the worry in her eyes and say gruffly, "Club Mafia is our home. It belongs to the five of us. Angelo built it when your father died and we all head there as a place of safety."

"All?"

"You could say it's a substitute Rockwell Academy." I chuckle at the expression on her face. "It's where we all live together as we did back then. It's well guarded and the only place any of us can truly relax."

"Will they be there?" She looks excited at the prospect, and I take great delight in nodding.

"They will. To be honest, they wanted us to go there before Sicily. Your friends are anxious to check you're ok."

"My friends." She sounds a little pensive, causing me to stare at her with concern.

She shrugs and says lightly, "I just wish I could remember."

"You will." I nod confidently. "The memory will return

when you spend time with them. Every single one played a part in bringing you home and made their own sacrifices on your behalf."

"I feel so bad." She looks worried and I shake my head. "Don't be. They found their own happily ever after and every single one of them married for love, not power."

"They're married." She regards me through wide eyes. "Because of me?"

I laugh softly. "It was always the plan, even before you were taken. We had it all worked out. Marry for power and take over the whole fucking corrupt world we live in. Become the masters of our own destinies and show our fathers how it's done."

"Who were you supposed to marry, Alessandro?"

I hate the pain in her eyes and I'm guessing she knows the answer to that already, as she says in a small voice. "Allegra?"

Sighing, I pull her close and whisper against her lips, "It wasn't decided, but one thing is guaranteed, the moment I met you I knew."

"What?" Her eyes are wide and filled with lust as I growl, "That you were my woman."

"No, you didn't." She shakes her head and laughs, and I growl, "And you felt it too."

She stares at me for a long minute and then says softly, "If I could remember the moment we first met, Alessandro, I'm certain that's true. However, I can't. All I've got is the moment I saw you when I opened my eyes in the hospital. I felt safe with you. There was an overwhelming need to be close to you and I suppose that answers your question. Yes, I knew, and I suppose if my memory returns, it will only confirm that."

Our lips meet against her last word and as we kiss, it stirs the beast inside me, and I thank fuck my grandfather equipped this jet with a bedroom. Tearing off my seatbelt, I do the same to hers and pull her hastily to the rear of the jet, where I doubt we'll leave for the rest of the journey.

The fact we pass my men, who always travel with me, causes Winter to blush with embarrassment, but they're used to scenes like this. Not with me, though, never with me.

As I tug her inside and slam the door, I glare at her with a hunger that she obviously shares because without another word, she shimmies out of her dress and stands before me naked and needy and with a low growl, I tear off my shirt and step out of my pants but before I can say or do anything at all, she drops to her knees before me.

CHAPTER 28

WINTER

There is only one thing I want, and he's standing before me naked and splendid, decorated in tribal ink and lust. My man is a beast and I love the untamed, rough exterior with the heart of an angel inside. I crawl on my knees toward him and love the lust that flares in his eyes as he stands like a conquering hero watching me. I don't care if I look like a wanton whore. I feel like one inside and as I reach him, I lick his feet, causing him to growl, "Fuck Winter, this is so hot."

I flip my long, black hair over my shoulder and work my way up his legs, biting, licking and rubbing my tits against them like the sluttiest pole dancer in the world. I reach his cock, already leaking at the tip, and I lick the salty liquid onto my tongue and close my eyes, moaning softly. He fists my hair and tugs down hard, making it hurt like crazy and I love how wild it makes me. As I take him in deep, I adore how smooth his shaft is against my tongue and as it hits the back of my throat, I lock my lips around it and suck like mad.

The tightening of his hold tells me he's so turned on and as he thrusts inside, it's almost degrading as he pumps inside me like a cheap whore. However, I want him to use me. I want to give him my everything because he makes me feel so hot and sexy, I would do anything to make him happy.

He roars as he releases a steady stream of hot salty cum down my throat, which I swallow with greed, loving how it marks me inside with his scent. Before I know what's happening, he reaches down and slings me over his shoulder and slaps my ass so hard I cry out with a mixture of pain and ecstasy.

He bites on my neck before throwing me heavily onto the bed and towers over me like a caveman who dragged his mate to his mud hut and when I see the feral gleam in his eyes, I should be afraid as he reaches down and removes his belt from his pants and slaps it against his thigh.

"Fuck me, Alessandro."

My voice sounds needy and edged in wantonness and he grabs my hands and binds them together above my head, threading the leather through the headboard and tightening it so I can't move.

My breath comes heavy and fast as the wet gush of heat settles between my thigh and as he drops to deal with that, I cry out as his tongue flits against my clit, and he forces my thighs so wide he sees the whole of me. This time he tortures me with his tongue, the pad of his thumb crushing my clit into submission. I wriggle and moan as he drives my body to extremes and only when I don't think I can take anymore, does he sheath his cock and slide inside, hard, fast and rough.

He slams into me, causing me to scream with a mixture of pain and pleasure. He makes no secret of the fact he is marking me as his, and I'm guessing no man would ever measure up to him, anyway. This isn't gentle love, it's fucking at its most depraved and I'm loving every minute of it. Over and over again, he slams into my wet heat, and I scream his name so hard I'm certain they hear it back in Sicily.

We explode together and as we ride the most fantastic high, I can recommend the mile high club because this is the most pleasant way to travel, the *only* way to travel and I know in my heart I never want to be anywhere else.

* * *

WE DON'T STOP. The remainder of the flight is spent exploring our respective bodies and making certain not one inch of skin goes unexplored. We talk, we laugh, and we discover shared dreams and by the time the seatbelt sign goes on, I could sleep for days.

I don't even care as we walk through the cabin, trying to ignore the curious glances of the soldiers who must have endured the flight from hell listening to us and as Alessandro straps me back into my seat, he laughs softly and gently nips on my ear, whispering, "Don't worry, the bedroom is sound-proofed."

"And you're just telling me that now."

I blush because it was obvious how embarrassed I was as we walked through the plane and Alessandro grins. "I didn't want them to think we were just sleeping back there. I have a reputation to protect."

"But you said…" I'm confused, and he places his finger on my lips and laughs softly. "That was placed on hold for two years. I'm guessing they were cheering me on because God knows I deserve every amazing minute of being deep inside you."

My eyes soften when I realize what he sacrificed for me, and I am so happy to return the favor. Knowing that I've never been with anyone but him is one memory I welcomed with opened arms. Just thinking of the man who called himself my husband makes me shiver with revulsion. It could have been so different and even though I know in my heart, he subjected me to all kinds of horrors, somehow, I think that would have been the worst he could do, and I am thankful I was spared an intimacy with him that makes my flesh creep.

* * *

CLUB MAFIA IS an impressive residence set in the middle of nowhere. As our helicopter circles the mansion, I stare down at a place I couldn't have imagined if I tried.

"It's beautiful."

Alessandro grips my hand and looks so emotional it brings tears to my eyes as he growls, "I have waited a long time to bring you home."

I have no words and crash my lips against his, just desperate for one more taste because there will never be enough of him to sate the thirst I have. We have so much time to make up and I pray that longing never dies.

The customary black cars are waiting and as we step outside onto the tarmac, I take a deep breath because even though Alessandro's home in Sicily screamed mafia, this one would eat it for breakfast.

The emotionless soldiers who hide behind black shade, all dressed in black suits with expressions that give nothing away. They are respectful yet emotionless and if I weren't accompanying an even darker soul, I would be shit scared right now.

Alessandro looks exactly what he is. A mafia heir in waiting. His long wild hair is tamed into his customary ponytail and his eyes are hidden behind the usual sunglasses. He wears black hand-tailored suits, paired with a black silk shirt, unfastened enough to reveal the dark script on his magnificent chest. He is so powerful in every way and just remembering how I crawled on my hands and knees to lick his feet, is turning me on again, making me anxious to deal with the formalities and fast.

Alessandro helps me inside the car and jumps in after me and we make the short journey through the magnificent grounds to the main house that appears to be guarded better than the Whitehouse. I shiver when I see the glint of steel in the distance, knowing there are several armed assassins waiting for somebody to step out of line.

We pull up outside a magnificent entrance and, as the door flies open, I steady my nerves for what happens next. A reunion of sorts. I'm supposed to know these people and I am praying to God and anyone else who will listen that I remember them and what they mean to me because if they are half the man Alessandro is, then it will be a very happy homecoming indeed.

CHAPTER 29

ALESSANDRO

It makes me so proud bringing Winter to Club Mafia. Now it's complete. We are all back together and I can't wait to discover what that means for her memory.

We head inside and I nod as Roberto meets us as always, and from the number of soldiers crowding every exit, I'm guessing we're the last to arrive.

This time Roberto doesn't direct us to the main hall. The one Angelo usually prefers to greet us. We are heading to a much more personal place that I'm anxious to visit with the woman holding my hand so tightly.

"Where are we going?"

She stares around her in awe, and I tease, "You'll see."

Her eyes widen as she senses a shock coming and I laugh softly. "Hopefully it will be a pleasant surprise, perhaps even something that will bring your memory back."

She appears curious and as we reach the end of the long marble tiled corridor, Roberto opens the door and announces our arrival.

"Mr. Majerio and Miss. Sontauro."

I don't do emotion but I'm experiencing every bit of it now, on hearing our names spoken out loud, announcing we're together at last. If I'm feeling it, God only knows what the people inside must be thinking and as we pass Roberto into the room, it's as if time has re-winded and we are back at our house at Rockwell Academy.

Every inch of it is exactly as we left it. The layout, the furniture, even the paint on the walls. It's a replica of the first home we ever shared together, and it's as if we're walking from the present straight back to the past.

Angelo looks up from the couch and grins, the pleasure in seeing his sister evident in his usually guarded eyes. He stands and I note Flynn watching from his usual position in the corner, crouching in his favorite chair, the emotion pushing away the madness in his eyes for once.

Ivan turns around from his preferred position in front of the television and Malik glances up from his laptop placed on the nearby table.

As we head inside, Angelo growls playfully, "What took you so long? We nearly ate all the pizza."

Winter tenses beside me and openly stares at the familiar scene. It's as if the past two years never happened as we are transported back in time. My friends have managed to even dress the same as they did back then, and it means a lot knowing they have gone to so much trouble.

Winter appears lost for words and for a moment, I think every person in this room holds their breath.

Then she says with a quiver in her voice, "Maybe someone had better call Emma from upstairs. Not Flynn though, promise me that at least."

As the tears spill from her eyes, I sense the relief from every last one of us. At least one thing worked. She remembers something and as Angelo reaches his sister, his arms wrap around her so tightly I'm sure she can't breathe. For a moment, we let them have this. Brother and sister-twins, where they should be, looking out for one another, ready to take on the world. There's a lump in my throat that shouldn't be there. I don't do emotion, which is noted by Ivan, who growls, "What's this? Have you become a weak pussy since we last met?"

He steps forward and thumps me playfully and as we hug it out, I don't ever want to be anywhere else than with these people, back in time when we still had everything to play for.

Winter

The relief is overwhelming. I remember. It's as if I only stepped out for a class and now I'm back with the men who mean the most to me in the world. They've always been my guys and I remember everything. The fights they had and the arrogance they wore like a favorite sweater. I remember being so angry when they tried to control me and yet I loved every last one of them for just being them.

When I saw Angelo heading toward me, I almost fell into his arms. It's so good to be back among the people I love, and I only wish I could shake the pain I'm living with right now. It's not over. I know that for fact, and I wish like crazy I could remember something that is so important to me.

As Angelo pulls away, another worried face comes into view, and I stare at Flynn with tears in my eyes.

"I won't break, you know."

He steps forward and wraps those strong arms around me much like my brother just did and as I hug him back hard, he whispers, "Good to have you home where you belong."

"I missed you, Flynn." I tighten my grip and he laughs softly.

"You're just saying that. I'm guessing you don't even remember me."

I pull away and stare up in astonishment because I do remember him, very well, in fact. I also remember a meeting where he was accompanied by a woman who looked a lot like Emma, and it confuses me a little and I say with a curious edge to my voice, "Did you marry Emma?" He laughs out loud and shakes his head. "Not quite, but Louisa shares certain similarities with her. What can I say? I have a type."

He winks, which causes me to grin, and then a rough arm drops around my shoulder and a low growl whispers in my ear, "My turn now."

Spinning around, I fall into Ivan's arms, and he brushes his lips against my cheek and whispers, "Welcome home, my angel."

"Thank you."

"For what?"

He says abruptly, reminding me he isn't one for sentiment.

"For helping me come home."

The ever-present tears stream down my face, which he wipes away with his fingers and says softly, "Did you really think you'd get away from us, angel? Your brother gave us strict instructions, remember?"

I nod, laughing, "I do remember. I remember how happy I was here living with you guys. Not all the time, but most of it."

I turn when another familiar face steps into view and I say slightly shyly, "Malik. It's good to see you."

Of all the guys, he is the least emotional, and it surprises me the most when he pulls me roughly into his arms and sighs with relief. "At last. Welcome home princess, we missed you."

As we hug it out, four more men force their way in, and we must look a disturbing sight all huddled together like a football team at the Super Bowl.

After a while, I say slightly breathlessly, "Did somebody say pizza?"

As the others drift off, one man remains and as I fall naturally by his side, I'm so happy I could cry. I'm back where I belong, with the people who love me the most but there is an overwhelming sadness that is reminding me this isn't over yet.

CHAPTER 30

ALESSANDRO

Watching Winter laugh again is the best sight in the world. For one night only we are the kids we were back at Rockwell. Chilling out, eating pizza and laughing, something that's been on short supply these past few years. It's as if the storm has broken and rain is drenching our battered souls. We did it; we brought down the madness that still goes by the name Massimo Delauren.

Winter laughs at something Flynn says, and I don't even mind that his arm is draped across her shoulders as he whispers his usual shit in her ears.

Angelo takes the seat beside me and throws me a beer. "Thank fuck it's all over."

"Are you sure about that?" He raises his eyes at my question, and I jerk my thumb in Winter's direction.

"She's still suffering."

"How?" Angelo's low growl matches how I feel inside, and I sigh heavily. "She's lost her memory and even though parts of it are resurfacing, there's still a lot of shit she'll have to deal with. Who knows what that fucker put her through and when she remembers, it may throw up a whole set of new problems."

"Do you really believe he has a normal brain?"

I roll my eyes and Angelo nods, casting a tortured look at his sister, who appears a lot happier now.

"We keep him alive and when Winter remembers what he did to her, we will have our revenge. There is not a chance in hell I will allow him the easy way out. He may not experience physical pain, but I will become a master at mental torture. If I do nothing else, I will make his last days on earth a living hell and he will pray for death to come and claim his twisted soul."

Malik drops down in the seat opposite and grins. "Everything went according to plan. Word on the street is that Massimo suffered a catastrophic stroke, reducing him to a vegetable. His daughter will inherit his wealth and her husband the business."

I look across at Ivan, who is listening to Flynn and Winter and as I catch his eye, he nods toward the door.

After excusing myself from my friends, I head over to Winter and my heart lurches when she lifts those beautiful eyes to mine, and it's like a physical dart to my heart. As I drop a light kiss on her lips, I whisper, "I won't be long."

"Where are you going?" She looks fearful, making me second guess my decision, but Flynn catches my eye and nods toward the door, mouthing, "I've got this."

Turning back to Winter, I run my finger down her cheek and say huskily, "You know Ivan, always spoiling for a fight."

She laughs softly and rolls her eyes. "Go and have your fun. I'll be right where you left me."

It's like a physical pain stabbing me as I walk away from her, but Ivan's right. I need this, he needs this and I'm guessing Winter needs this because the sooner we get back to normal, the better it will be for everyone.

* * *

"That we will deal with." Angelo's voice is rough and filled with warning because he will do anything to keep that smile on Winter's face. "What's she said?"

I shrug. "Just that there's something important she can't shake. It's as if something is blocking her memory and it's vital she remembers."

Angelo shrugs. "It's understandable. I mean, I've never lost my memory, even though I've wished it countless times."

"You don't mean that. It's the past that makes us determined to do better in the future."

Angelo shakes his head. "We've all lived with shit, and I can't see that changing anytime soon. It's how you deal with it that matters now."

"Talking of shit. What are you going to do with Massimo?"

I'm interested because I believe his stay at my grandfather's home will be a short one, and Angelo grins.

"Tomorrow, a plane is taking him back to Los Angeles. There's an institution that has his name on one of the doors."

"An institution?"

Angelo grins. "It's where madness lives. A hospital of sorts for patients who can no longer care for themselves. Massimo will fit right in, and I've reserved him a spot with ordinary people surrounding him, which he will absolutely hate. He will be kept alive for as long as possible with only the odd visit from yours truly to bring him up to date on how happy his 'wife' is with her new husband while they live in his home and profit from his business."

"And?"

It's not enough and Angelo shrugs. "You can always pile on the misery by visiting him yourself. I have been assured by the doctors there is nothing they can do for him. He is permanently paralyzed and in a state of locked-in syndrome. He can't even eat and will be fed through a tube for the rest of his miserable life, and yet his brain functions normally."

I follow Ivan to the gym and as we walk, he growls, "Fuck, I need to let off steam."

"You have a wife for that."

He laughs out loud. "Do you honestly think I want to do this to my wife? You're one sick bastard."

"I heard she can fight."

I grin as Ivan rolls his eyes. "Charlotte believes she can do a lot of things, but her fighting skills are basic level. She has more cultivated ones that interest me more."

"Where is she?"

"With the others. Angelo wanted tonight to be about Winter. To ease her back into our lives gently and try to make her feel safe and loved. She'll get to meet the women tomorrow, but for one night only, we're heading back to the past and I can't wait to find out how complacent you've become."

We reach the gym and waste no time in ripping off our clothes and enter the ring naked, save for our Calvin Klein's.

As we circle one another, It's as if a huge weight has lifted because now, in this moment, I can channel my aggression and let off some steam.

The first blow hits me hard and my breath is winded in my body as Ivan growls, "You're a little rusty, Beast."

In answer, I swipe my fist and catch him low in the stomach, but he merely laughs before kicking my legs from under me, causing me to slam down hard on the ground.

For a few painful moments The Savage reminds The Beast what it's like to lose and, with an angry roar, I gather my mind and focus on the only thing I need right now. My rage.

As we slug it out, it's not pretty, and the air becomes thick with blood and perspiration. The agonized roars and feral groans disturbing the usual peace as we batter one another in a much-needed show of aggression that I've been holding onto since Winter left.

As we brawl like backstreet fighters, it clears my head and

brings with it the realization that Ivan was always the only man who could beat me. He is obviously fighting his own demons and with every punch, every kick and every blood coated bruise, it regenerates our souls and reminds us exactly who we are. We will always need each other. We are evenly matched and have our own set of rules. It's good to be handed my ass from time to time, and I will only accept that from him.

Time has no meaning in the ring and as the last punch falls, we groan on the floor, battered and bloodied but so high on adrenalin I would go again if my body could take it.

"Fuck, I needed that."

Ivan gasps beside me and I nod in agreement. "It's been a long time, Savage."

"Too long."

"So, what's it like to head up a family, especially one as fucked up as Massimo's?"

Ivan pulls himself up and leans against the ropes, and I follow him as he laughs softly. "It's good man. Those fuckers can't believe their luck. The tales they tell are of one fucked up pile of shit."

"I don't even want to hear them."

He says with concern. "They hated their boss and what he was capable of."

"Like what?"

"His hobbies mainly. He had an endless supply of young men delivered for his own pleasure. He strung them up in his dungeons and fucked with their minds and bodies."

I feel sick and he growls, "Word is, he had his own private part of the house nobody had access to. Only his fingerprint opened the doors, and he had a silent army to serve him."

"Silent?"

"He removed their tongues so they couldn't speak of the horrors they witnessed."

Just picturing Winter in that hellish place twists the knife even deeper into my soul and Ivan says with disgust, "Nobody knows what really went on in there and I'm guessing the only one who does is blocking it from her mind."

"Do you think it's fear keeping her memory away?"

"Trauma, definitely. Charlotte told me she read up on it."

I snort and he rolls his eyes. "Of course, she would, but she said anything could trigger the memory and when it returns, it may not be a pleasant one and we should be prepared for that."

I consider his words and I suppose I always knew of that possibility. Winter may be here physically, but mentally she's still fighting to find her way back to us and I'm not sure any of us are really prepared to deal with what happens when she does.

CHAPTER 31

WINTER

*A*ngelo slides in beside me and Flynn nods respectfully. "Can I fetch you a drink, Winter? Non-alcoholic of course, boss's orders."

He grins as I giggle, loving how good they always make me feel. Being here, back at Rockwell, in my mind at least, it's as if the past never happened and we can finally look forward to the future.

As Flynn heads off, Angelo drapes his arm around my shoulders, and I rest my head on him like we always used to do.

"How are you?"

He sounds anxious and I smile softly. "Good, thanks. It's a dream being back here. I may not remember the details, but I know my life was a horror show."

"Do you remember anything?"

I think about his question and shiver. I'm scared to delve too deep because of the monster lurking around the corner that may just destroy me if I get too close and my voice shakes. "I'm scared of the past, Angelo."

His hold tightens around my shoulder, and he growls

ominously. "Nothing can hurt you now. You have hell's soldiers fighting your corner."

"I know."

I sigh heavily. "Sometimes a flash of something painful hits me when I least expect it. I am always fearing being punished. I can't even glance at myself in a mirror, and I guess it's because I won't like what I find."

"What do you mean?" Angelo's tone is even, but I sense the anger radiating from inside him and I whisper. "I may have become a monster to survive. What if I remember and can't live with what I've done?"

"If you did anything, it was because you had no choice which is something we all live with. Fight or flight, as they say, and so you only had one option."

He turns to face me. "Mafia isn't an occupation they list as a career option. It's a business that only a select few can master. We were born into this life and have suffered because of it. We are products of it, and it has molded our souls. We do what we must to get through the day and the darkest nights and I'm guessing that if you did anything, it was with that in mind. When we heard our father murder our mother, it was just another day at the office. Flynn, Ivan, Malik and Alessandro, also bear the scars of who we are. Our life isn't normal and never will be. We operate in madness and do what we must to survive. The fact you are here now tells me how incredibly brave you are. If you wake up one day and stare at a memory that returns, face it with courage, knowing that it can't beat you. You conquered fear and fought your way back to us and so don't cower away from your memories because they are what brought you back to us."

Just hearing my brother's usual strong words, give me the reassurance I so badly need. Yes, we have dealt with more in a short life than many ever witness, and I suppose he's right. It's made us stronger. Whatever happened in the two years since I left will not make a fairy-tale, more like a horror story. I have no doubt about that and so I grip hold of a firm resolve to face whatever memory is waiting for me and understand that whatever happened was merely a fight for survival.

Malik heads our way and stares at me with concern.

"I'm sorry, Winter."

"What for?"

"For taking so long to set you free."

He looks angry and I'm guessing it's at himself more than anything, and I remember how he always prided himself on being in control. The man who was always one step ahead of the rest, second guessing events before they could affect us.

"It's not your fault." I smile and then say firmly, "I may not remember much, but I couldn't have prevented what happened."

He sits and says with interest. "So, do you remember anything at all?"

"Not much. Vague memories come back to me and then go as quickly as they came. It's as if everything is out of focus in my mind. I can sense them, but don't see the full picture."

I sigh heavily. "I suppose that's better than nothing. When something happens to jog that memory, I can remember it as clearly as when it happened. But I need something to prompt it. When I walked in here, the scene was familiar. I knew everything. I remembered how happy I was here, and everything swam into focus. If you ask me about what happened when I left, though, I couldn't tell you."

I glance across at Angelo and say anxiously, "Everything's a blur. I suppose my mind has blocked things out for a reason, but there is an overwhelming sense of something sinister waiting."

"Can you remember anything about what happened with Massimo?"

Malik voices what I'm guessing they all want to know and Angelo growls, "It's too soon."

I shake my head and smile. "It's fine. Please ask me anything because it may just help trigger a memory. Strangely, I remember nothing except I was so scared. Even now I peer over my shoulder, fearful of something I'm not certain of. I have an overwhelming need to hide, to remain invisible and to keep quiet. It somehow feels wrong even speaking, as if I don't have permission and I have no desire to see my reflection, almost as if I won't like what's there."

"You're afraid of looking in a fucking mirror." Angelo growls with a slow burning rage and I sigh heavily. "When I was in the hospital, there was a mirror in the bathroom. I ignored it. I suppose I was afraid of what I might find in my reflection. When I stayed at Alessandro's grandfather's house, there were mirrors everywhere. Again, I tried not to look and if I did catch a glimpse, I quickly looked away. I'm not sure why, but I am fearful of being punished if I speak, or even glance at anything, myself included. It's always there, as if I'm waiting for something bad to happen, even though I'm now in safe hands."

Malik looks thoughtful.

"I'll do some digging. Massimo has many enemies, not all of whom ended their days chained to his dungeon walls."

For some reason, his words cause a flicker of something that's a lot like ice running through my veins, immobilizing my extremities, and making it difficult to breathe.

I must gasp because Angelo says quickly, "What?"

I just stare into my mind and am so cold, I shiver and the only thing I can make out were the steel bars of a cage.

Malik's voice joins me there and he whispers, "What do you see?"

"Darkness." I shiver as if I'm chilled to the bone and my teeth chatter as I whisper, "It's so dark. I'm so cold." Malik's smooth voice encourages me to dig a little deeper. "Is anybody with you?"

"No. I'm alone and I'm sitting on a swing in a cage. I have nothing on. I'm naked on a swing, and I'm locked in."

Angelo curses beside me and Malik's deep voice says firmly, "What else?"

As the memory returns, I can sense the tears falling down my face as I say sadly, "I was his prisoner. The cage was my home until he came for me."

As I glance up, the image fades and I lean back against the couch and smile through my tears. "I remembered something. That must be a good sign, surely."

The anger on their faces wraps me in safety. Knowing I have their full protection chases the demons away and I say brightly, "It's not so bad. At least I was alone and, the good news is I wasn't his loving wife."

Turning to Angelo, I need to know. "Please tell me I wasn't his wife and that my memory isn't playing tricks on me."

Malik interrupts. "Alessandro told me what you said, and I investigated further. There is no record of any marriage between you and Massimo Delauren. In fact, you are not listed on any database at all in connection to him."

The relief is almost overwhelming and drives away the fear from a few moments earlier.

"Thank God."

I smile happily. "When I saw him at Alessandro's grandfather's house..."

"What the fuck?" Angelo looks horrified and I rest my hand on his arm and say firmly, "I needed to. I wanted to face the monster, and I had the best protection by my side."

Angelo doesn't seem convinced, but Malik appears interested.

"What happened?"

"I knew he wasn't my husband. Don't ask me how, it was

just a certainty that was never in any doubt. We were never intimate, thank God, and all I had was a burning hatred for the man who sat before me."

Angelo looks as if I've stabbed him with a knife as he says through gritted teeth, "I never wanted you to be in the same room as him again."

"It was necessary." A little of the fire returns to my voice as I challenge my twin. "In order to fight, I need every weapon I can get. Before seeing him, he was just a name, a fearful memory and the monster in the shadows. When I witnessed how he is now, it neutralized the fear in an instant. He can't hurt me again and the table has turned. Now we have the power, and it was the one thing I was sure of."

"What?" Malik is quick to ask, and I say with anger controlling my voice, "He needs to live to suffer for what he did. A slow and agonizing death because something's telling me even that is too good for him."

The pride in Angelo's eyes makes me smile and then he turns to Malik and growls, "See what you can find out. I want to discover everything about Massimo and his life. There must be something we can use to torture him with. That man will learn what it's like to be the victim for once and this time death will not be an option. We will make him pay for what he did to my sister, and I'm counting on you to come up with the best way to make that happen."

Malik nods and it makes me smile, witnessing the look they share. There they are, my mafia warriors and Angelo is right. Far from fearing who I am and what I became, I should celebrate the fact that it's made me the survivor I needed to be.

CHAPTER 32

ALESSANDRO

We drag our sorry asses back to the others and the look of horror on Winter's face makes us all laugh. I suppose we do look a sight as the bruises develop and the blood smears across our naked chests.

Malik rolls his eyes as Flynn grins and shouts, "Who won?"

"We all did." I smile as I drop beside my woman and love the lust that sparks in her eyes as I take her hand.

"We are all winners here. Wouldn't you agree, baby?"

She nods. "I most definitely agree with that."

She seems concerned. "Are you hurt?"

Ivan snorts from across the room as he tosses me a beer. "Childs play."

She rolls her eyes. "I see it's business as usual."

"It's been a long time."

I wince as I catch a sore spot, and Winter shakes her head. "When will you ever grow up?"

She fixes Ivan with a stern expression. "You should know better. Save it for your enemies, not each other."

"Where's the fun in that?" He drops her a wink, and she turns to me and shakes her head. "I'll never understand you;

either of you. Why put yourselves through this? It doesn't make sense?"

Flynn shrugs. "They use it to let off steam and I'm guessing they're both feeling better now because of it. Me, I prefer sex. What can I say? I'm a lover, not a fighter, and I always will be."

Malik twists his lips into his evil grin. "We all have our preferred method of release."

"I dread to think what yours is." I growl at him, and he shrugs. "I get no complaints."

"That's because they probably can't recall it."

Flynn digs and Malik nods. "That can be one of the side effects, but I'm working on it."

"What are you even talking about?"

Winter looks confused and Angelo says with a grin, "It's best you don't ask. Malik prefers to torture his partners first. He calls it foreplay. Well, at least it is for him."

Winter shivers beside me and it makes me laugh as I whisper, "Talking of which."

She throws me a warning stare and then looks anxiously at her brother, who just looks slightly nauseous and sighs heavily. "Perhaps we should leave it there. It's late and we can catch up in the morning."

Flynn nods. "All this talk of sex is making me hungry."

We stare at him in confusion, and he laughs softly. "But my hunger is not for food. I have a wife now and one of the perks of that is…"

"Goodnight, Flynn." Angelo interrupts and nods toward the door. "I'll come with you. I believe Louisa is with Jasmine and Charlotte."

Winter says quickly, "They're here?"

Angelo nods. "We wanted tonight to be all about us. A trip down memory lane you could call it. You'll meet them in the morning. They can't wait."

Winter smiles. "I'd like that. If anything, just to offer them my commiserations. Do they even know what they've taken on?"

Flynn laughs out loud. "They don't call me The Angel for nothing. Louisa is living the dream right now."

We all laugh as Angelo grabs him by the arm and pulls him from the room and Ivan stands and cracks his knuckles. "I'm glad Charlotte is so interested in medicine. Maybe she can find a nurse's uniform and tend to my wounds."

He winks as he heads off, and I can only imagine the horror on his pretty wife's face when she sees his battered and bloodied body.

Malik looks after him thoughtfully and then sighs.

"I must head off, too. I have information to learn, and it may take me all night. It's good to see you home where you belong, Winter, and if you remember anything at all, let me know."

He heads off and Winter shakes her head. "I'll never understand what goes on inside that man's mind. I pity the woman he marries; she will need to be made of strong stuff."

I must agree with her there because Malik enjoys serious shit that the rest of us couldn't even begin to wrap our heads around.

Winter looks at me with concern.

"Does it hurt anywhere?"

I wince and point to my chest. "I think he bruised my ribs."

She twists her lips into a wicked grin and before I can see where she's going with this, she presses her lips to the purple bruise developing at a rapid rate.

"Does this make it better?" She whispers against my skin, and I nod. "A little."

She moves down my body, her tongue trailing a path, causing my cock to wake up and remind me he's been underused lately.

"What about here?"

She swirls her tongue against my navel and then her fingers

pull down the band of my pants, releasing my eager cock into the room.

"That hurts the most." I growl and as she slides my cock deep into her mouth, I groan out loud.

Lying back against the cushion with Winter buried deep between my thighs, I could be in heaven right now. Watching her head bob up and down as she sucks, teases and licks my shaft, I give way to the sensations she creates. Her willing fingers cup my balls and massage them as she sucks and as I lie back and enjoy the sweetest attention, I can't believe my fucking luck.

As I come hard and shoot a steady stream down her throat, I swear I see stars and as she licks my shaft clean and pulls my pants back up, her eyes are loaded and heavy with lust as she grabs my hand and whispers, "It's time for bed and if I get one wink of sleep tonight, I'll be disappointed."

She grins, and that's all I need to move me to my feet fast and tug her after me as if the house is on fire.

* * *

WE HEAD to my room and as we enter the dark space, she peers around with curiosity. The room is huge and dressed in charcoal and silver, the silk bedding calling our names from the emperor sized bed set in the middle of the room. The golden glow of concealed lighting creates a seductive atmosphere and just the fluttering of the drapes at the window indicate the cool breeze outside is waiting patiently to caress our heated skin.

Without a word, Winter shrugs out of her clothes to match my own state of undress and just seeing her swaying slightly in the dusky light of the room makes me openly stare in wonder.

She flicks her long ebony hair over one shoulder, and it caresses her bare breast, causing my cock to twitch and she whispers huskily, "What are you waiting for?"

In two short strides, I reach for her hand and tug her hard into my body and growl, "I can be soft, or I can be considerate. I can make this slow, sensuous, and full of love, or I can fuck you until you can't walk. Your choice."

The way her eyes flash and her breathing intensify, tells me my answer before her words dust the air. "Fuck me hard Alessandro. I need The Beast tonight."

As I grasp her hair in one hand, I tug it down firmly so her face lifts to mine and the fire I see burning in her eyes matches my own as I devour her lips with a hunger I doubt will ever be satiated.

It's never enough though and pushing her roughly toward the wall, I kick her legs apart and force her back, loving the wild passion in her eyes as I growl, "I want to hear you scream, baby. Tell the world you're mine."

With one thrust I am inside her, bareback and in heaven. Her moan of desire greets me as I push in hard and deep, loving how her slick walls clench my cock and own it like she always has. Her ass scrapes against the wall as I hammer her to it and as I suck and bite her neck, her scream of pleasure stokes the fire inside me.

This is fucking at its most basic and is the only thing we need right now. It's a desperate act of two mates who lost one another and then found themselves again. One night only will turn into a lifetime and now she is back with me, it begins now.

As she comes all over my cock, she screams my name, and my roar of ecstasy dives out of the open window and tells the world who they're up against. Nobody will ever tell me I can't have this woman and anyone that tries better run for cover because I will never give her up all the time I breathe, and if my grandfather, or anyone else has a problem with that, they can go and fuck themselves.

CHAPTER 33

WINTER

I have so much time to make up with Alessandro. It's like a physical ache that won't decline. When he leaves me, I am waiting for him to return. I always want him beside me, almost as if I can't operate when he's not around.

When he left with Ivan, I experienced a physical pull to go and find him. It scares me a little because I shouldn't be dependent on a man so soon. Maybe it's because he was the first person I saw when I woke up. Or it could be something stronger than that. It's as if I was always meant to be by his side and I'm guessing it started at Rockwell Academy.

Alessandro runs us a deep, hot bath, in the awesome bathroom attached to his room. The tub is black, and the taps are gold. Some may say it's garish. I love it. The black towels look brand new and the dark travertine tiles are warm beneath my feet. Subtle lighting creates a welcoming ambiance and if I could, I would lock the door and stay here for the foreseeable future.

Club Mafia is my happy place because *they* are here. The men I will dedicate my life to who have proven their loyalty more than I dared wish for.

Every single one of them holds a special place in my heart and as I sit in front of Alessandro, with the deep water lapping around us, I lean back and sigh with contentment.

As he soaps away the day, I say softly, "Moments don't come more perfect than this one."

His low laugh settles against my ear. "This is your perfect moment? Here I am thinking it was when I fucked you hard against the wall."

I giggle, loving hearing the sound. I can't remember the last time I heard it and as I nestle into those strong, powerful arms, I whisper, "I love you, Alessandro."

He stills behind me and then his lips graze my neck and as I turn to face him, I stare into two pools of tenderness I wasn't expecting to see. His lips brush against mine and he says softly, "Ti amo, baby girl."

He deepens the kiss and as the water laps against us, our tongues clash and our hearts beat faster. Words are unnecessary in the heat of the moment.

He fists my hair and holds my head in place and as he devours my aching lips, it's as if I'm balancing on the edge of heaven. I feel his cock rock hard against my stomach, and with a wicked smile, I pull back and shift so I'm straddling him, my breasts dragging against his chest as the water rains down them. As I slide on top of him, his groan of pleasure matches my own and just the sensation of him inside me causes my heart to go into freefall. As I cup his handsome face, I stare with a hunger that will never get old at the man of my dreams who woke me from a nightmare.

Slowly, I move up and down, staring into his eyes the entire time, and it's the most amazing experience in the world. I am making love to my man, and I never expected it to be so good.

He cups my chin and forces my lips to his and the leisurely way he tastes me makes me moan into his mouth and breaking away, he drops his head and takes my nipple into his mouth and rolls it around his tongue, while pulling me in harder from behind.

I am officially in heaven as I fuck Alessandro in the tub and the sound of the water lapping over the edge adds drama to an occasion that really doesn't need any.

Rather than give into the orgasm that's never far away, I whisper, "Bed. Now!"

His low chuckle makes me grin as we step from the tub, dripping with water and need. Then we head straight into the bedroom to drench the silk sheets with a lot more than the water dripping from our bodies.

I lie back and stretch out my hands over my head as he settles between my thighs and forces them as wide as possible. I feel incredibly sexy right now and not embarrassed, as I always thought I would. Sex with Alessandro is an act of nature that will happen despite the obstacles thrown in our way and as he licks my need from deep inside me, I gasp at the pure pleasure that drips between my thighs.

"You taste so sweet, baby."

His muffled groan makes me smile and as he spreads me wider and sucks my clit, I don't ever want this to end. So many emotions are playing out right now and none of them include fear. How can I fear anything when I'm with him? He's everything to me, and I only feel safe when he's around.

As he works his way up my body, he bites, licks and sucks every inch of my skin and as he reaches my mouth, I love how I taste on his lips. Then, staring into my eyes, he slides in deep and the intensity flashing in his dark, turbulent eyes should scare me, but they only wrap me in comfort because I'm with him.

We fuck, we talk, and we fuck again. The night turns to day and, true to his word, sleep has played no part in this.

I don't think there is one part of him I don't explore and as I circle the scar on his chest just above his heart, I whisper, "How did this happen?"

"Club Mafia."

His low, husky voice sends a shiver down my spine as I look at the raised edges and gently press my lips to honor it.

"Tell me what happened."

He twirls my hair in his fingers as I stare into his eyes, and he grins. "The night you left we made a vow."

"We?"

He nods. "The five of us and Baron came along for the ride."

"Baron?" The name seems familiar and he can obviously sense my mind working because he waits for me to speak.

"I know that name."

"What do you know?"

"He saved me."

"How?" Alessandro looks confused and I smile at the memory that probably saved my life.

"I'm not sure how, but it was his words that kept me going. I can hear them now as clear as the day he said them."

As I stare into Alessandro's eyes, it's another man's face I see, back at the party when he offered me his advice. I am transported back to Rockwell and know those words were the most meaningful of my life, and I repeat them to Alessandro.

"Learn how to survive and always look for their weakness because there always is one. Then use that to your advantage to get what you want. The element of surprise is a powerful weapon, and I'm guessing you can learn to wield it where it will do the most damage."

"I don't understand." He appears confused and I smile happily, remembering the conversation as if it were yesterday.

"We were talking about my life after Rockwell Academy. I was afraid of what the future held and confided in him about my fears. I was resigned to the fact I couldn't change my future, and those words were his response to that. Somehow, I have repeated those words like a mantra for the past two years, always looking for my opportune moment. Then it happened."

"What do you remember?" Alessandro's voice is measured, but his eyes glitter with rage as I drag out another dark part of my soul into the light.

"I remember the confusion. A restaurant perhaps. Massimo was angry; there was chaos everywhere. He was distracted, he was never distracted, and I remember telling myself this was it. The opportune moment to escape, and so I took the box from his jacket that was hanging on the chair, knowing that whatever was concealed in the syringe would be potentially lethal. I didn't even stop to think and while he was shouting, I drove the needle straight into his neck."

I exhale sharply. "I was so scared, Alessandro. It was as if I could die at any moment, and then there is no recollection of what happened after that."

He nods. "You fell. He stumbled toward you, and took you down with him, hitting your head on the table as you went down."

"So, it was me."

I am strangely euphoric as I stare with delight into his eyes. "I brought him down, just like Baron promised me I could. My opportune moment tipped the balance and set me free. I remember."

The relief is enormous as I register what I did. Nobody else. Me. It's an indescribable sensation knowing I am the one responsible for my freedom and it empowers me in a way I wasn't expecting. It's as if the fog clears and I step into the sunshine. Tearing free from the chains holding me in place. I was the master of my own destiny and yet…"

I must frown because Alessandro says with concern, "What is it?"

"I don't know." I stare at him with confusion.

"I should be happy. It's over. I won."

"It is."

He smiles his reassurance, but there's something heavy weighing me down inside. An ache that grows stronger by the day that is promising to burst my bubble in a devastating way.

Trying to shake it from my head, I force a smile onto my face.

"It's good. All is good. Anyway, finish your story. Tell me about the scar."

I trace my fingers over the jagged edges and love how imperfect it is. Much like him, beautiful in its madness.

"We simulated removing our hearts for the battle ahead."

I wasn't expecting that, and I stare at him in shock. "You did what?"

He laughs softly. "Flynn had a claw shaped blade and one by one we scratched our skin deep enough to draw blood and as the blood spilled onto the paper, we signed a contract in blood to bring you home to us."

"Oh my god." I'm so shocked and he shrugs as if it was of no consequence.

"We all did it. We called it The Contract and the most important mission in life after Rockwell was setting about bringing you home."

"How?"

"Marrying for power. One by one, we would marry into rival families to make an army. The hardest thing of all was waiting for the plan to come together, knowing you were suffering with him."

He looks so tormented my heart physically hurts and I drop a light kiss on his lips and whisper, "Thank you."

He kisses me deeply with an intensity that heats my blood, knowing how far they were prepared to go to rescue me.

The time for talking is put on hold because it's actions that count now and this time we make love with an intensity that shocks me a little because being here with Alessandro at last dulls the pain of my past.

CHAPTER 34

ALESSANDRO

I leave Winter to sleep while I shower and change. I have calls to make and want to catch up with my brothers before the day runs away with us.

As I leave, I take a lingering glance at the sleeping beauty in my bed and still can't believe my luck. She loves me. The moment those words fell from her lips, it healed my soul. Nothing else matters now. My grandfather, Allegra and the Giodanos. Nothing but making Winter my wife and taking over the Majerio family as soon as required.

It will be a fight to the death to keep Winter by my side, but my grandfather chose me as his successor for a reason and I didn't miss the pride in his eyes whenever I stood up to him, despite the frown on his face. I am more like him than he would care to admit and I'm guessing he would be disappointed if I married Allegra, anyway.

I head outside and nod to the ever-present soldiers who guard our headquarters well. Their loyalty is to Club Mafia when they are here, not only their respective Don. Here Angelo is the Don, and we all offer him that respect, regardless of what and who we control in the outside world.

Stepping over to the fountain that is the centerpiece of the courtyard, I call my grandfather more out of respect than anything else.

"Alessandro."

His husky voice reaches out and grabs my attention and he says slowly, *"I trust you are in a more amenable frame of mind now you have had your fun."*

"Nothing has changed, Grandfather. I won't marry Allegra and will bring Winter home, or we remain here."

"Which is…"

Nobody knows about Club Mafia except those who belong and serve it, so I laugh softly.

"Here is here. That's all you need to know."

There's a brief silence before he sighs heavily.

"You put me in an unfortunate position with Don Giodano."

"You will find a way out of it."

"No, Alessandro."

"No, what?"

"I will do nothing. I will leave it up to you to explain why you are declaring war on the Giodano family. Because that's exactly what it will be if you back out of our deal. A bloodthirsty, desperate war where nobody wins. Ask yourself if she's worth it when you can have it all, anyway."

"The answer will always be yes. She's worth it and if it involves a war, it won't be the first one I've fought for her."

His exasperated sigh tells me he's disappointed in my reaction, but I can't worry about that.

His deep voice hisses back, *"Three months and the clock is ticking. I have every faith in you to do the right thing for everyone concerned."*

He cuts the call, giving me no chance to retaliate and I huff with frustration and light a cigarette to calm myself the fuck down.

An amused laugh hits me from behind and as I turn, I see Flynn sitting on the wall watching me.

"Jesus, Flynn, how long have you been stalking me?"

"My whole life, brother."

He winks as he points to my smoke.

"Got a spare?"

"You begging for leftovers now? Don't you have more money these days?"

He shrugs. "Louisa hates smoking."

I raise my eyes. "And the real reason is?"

"That is the real reason."

It makes me laugh out loud as I hand him a smoke and grin. "The Angel has been pussy whipped. I never thought I'd see the day."

'I'm not the only one judging by that conversation."

As I lean against the fountain, I shake my head. "She knows nothing. It was my decision."

I growl irritably, "If my grandfather believes I'll give up the only woman I have ever loved for a cold, emotionless, mafia princess who craves power and doesn't care who she has to marry to get it, he doesn't know me at all."

"So, you're about to fight another war. I can loan you my army if you like."

"I figured you might." We share a grin and I watch as he hops off the wall and saunters across, flicking the lit cigarette into the fountain after only one puff. "Dirty habit."

He grins. "You should get Malik onto your problem. Stuff like that gives him an orgasm. He'll thank you for it."

I consider our mysterious Arab friend and say with interest, "How is he coping with life in the family business?"

Flynn shrugs. "The same as the rest of us, I guess. He doesn't talk much about it but the tortured pain in his eyes deepens every time we meet."

"I noticed."

Tossing my own butt into the fountain, I jerk my thumb toward the house. "Let's eat. I'm keen to meet the woman who was mad enough to wear your wedding ring."

I note the softening expression of my chaotic friend and am happy he's found love. It's obvious because I've never seen him so calm and as we head inside, I am looking forward to introducing my woman to the others.

Flynn must be reading my mind because he says in a low voice, "How is she?"

As I picture her sucking my cock not that long ago, I grin. "She's perfect."

Flynn's eyes narrow and he fixes me with a stern gaze. "I wouldn't make it so obvious unless you want Angelo to cut you a new pair."

"He's good. Even welcomed me to the family."

Flynn whistles. "Then he's madder than I am."

As we head into the kitchen, I make straight for the coffee machine and hear. "Hey, baby."

Spinning around, I see a pretty girl head straight into Flynn's arms and for some reason it makes me smile when I witness the happiness on both their faces.

"Louisa."

At the sound of my voice, she turns and looks at me awkwardly, a blush staining her cheeks as she mutters, "Oh, um, hi…"

"Alessandro."

I smile to put her at ease, but Flynn adds. "The Beast to everyone else. More like a puppy dog, really."

As I fix him with my most ferocious glare, I don't miss the way her skin pales as she gazes between us with concern.

Flynn merely rolls his eyes and, taking her hand, pulls her over to me.

Stepping forward, I kiss her on both cheeks and whisper, "If you ever need help with him, call someone else. He's beyond any I can offer him."

I wink as she giggles, relaxing a little and my heart lifts when a sleepy looking woman heads into the room, barefoot and wearing one of my t-shirts.

Her hair is messy, and she yawns deeply and yet as soon as she sees me her face lights up and I don't miss the lust that sparks in her eyes.

Flynn sighs, causing her to spin around and the faint blush to her face when she sees Louisa and Flynn watching her with amusement, makes her say quickly, "I'm sorry, forgive my appearance but the aroma of coffee enticed me in here."

Flynn laughs out loud. "You have never looked more perfect, Angel. Come and meet Louisa, my wife."

A huge smile breaks across Winter's face and she steps forward and, to all our surprise, hugs Louisa close and for a moment I wonder if she's confusing her with her friend Emma who lived with us at Rockwell. Flynn had a thing for her, and it ended as they always did as one night only.

She pulls away and says with tears glistening in her eyes, "Thank you so much."

"For what?" Louisa appears confused and Winter says softly, "For making Flynn so happy and for helping bring me home."

Louisa appears a little emotional. "I'm so happy it all worked out."

Winter nods and, looking past her, catches my eye and I swear if we were alone, I would be inside her right now. "It's good to be back."

I hand her a coffee before slipping my arm around her shoulder and pull her close, leaning down and breathing in the sweet soft scent of my woman.

It's typical that Angelo chooses this moment to walk in, hand in hand with Jasmine, and the amusement on her face is the opposite of the frown on his.

Winter makes to move, but I keep a firm hold on her and growl, "Morning guys."

Jasmine grins wickedly as Angelo sighs, before his expression softens and he heads straight for Winter and plucks her from my side. As his own arms wrap around his sister, I can almost taste their emotion as they block out the rest of the room and enjoy the fact they are back together again.

I watch as the tears blur in Jasmine and Louisa's eyes as they stare at a scene I'm not sure any of us believed we'd see again, and it's only when Malik glides into the room that they pull apart when he says briskly, "I've spent an interesting night delving into Massimo's past and you may be interested in what I found."

We all stare at him with eager expressions and Angelo nods toward the door. "We'll talk over breakfast. I have a feeling this will be a long conversation." As we head off, it strikes me that Malik must have discovered something good because even he looks excited, and I hope that whatever it turns out to be is a good thing and won't interfere with the happiness we are enjoying right now.

CHAPTER 35

WINTER

*E*ven though I love my family and I consider Club Mafia to be that family, I only really want to be with Alessandro. It's as if we have so much time to make up for and I wish I was nestled in his arms, skin on skin, feeding him breakfast instead of attending a family one. The fact I'm underdressed hasn't escaped anyone's notice and I'm guessing I look a wreck due to my aversion to looking in the mirror.

There are still many puzzle pieces to slot into place and as we take our seats, I love that Alessandro's hand runs up and under the t-shirt and teases my bare pussy that is always so wet for him.

I shift awkwardly as Angelo smiles on my other side and leans in. "We should spend the morning together. We have a lot of catching up to do."

The fact that Alessandro's finger is now massaging my clit momentarily distracts me and I say slightly breathlessly, "Of course. I can't wait."

Jasmine catches my eye and smiles reassuringly, and I am looking forward to spending time with her, too. She is my family now, along with Louisa, and it's good to have female company at last.

It's obvious the two women adore their husbands. Even the short time I've spent with them tells me that. I don't miss the lingering looks and lustful glances that they share, and I'm happy Angelo and Flynn are happy at last. Angelo in particular is not only my brother but my best friend too and even the fact my memory has deserted me doesn't change that. It's as if I knew immediately. We share a deep connection that runs in our blood and that will never change.

"It's about time."

Flynn says with a growl, and I hear the harsh accent of our Russian friend say crossly, "Nobody set a time for this. You're lucky we made it at all."

"For fuck's sake, Ivan, don't embarrass me."

I'm surprised to detect a different accent and from the amusement on everyone's faces, there's a reason for that and as I turn to witness it for myself, I blink in astonishment.

I can't help the loud gasp that makes it from deep inside, and the room spins as I look at a face from my nightmares.

"What is it, baby?"

Alessandro's words cut through the lifting fog and my voice shakes as I try to form a sentence. "I… I… I…"

The atmosphere shifts and the tears blind me as I stare at a memory that hits me hard.

Standing before me larger than life is a living work of art. I've seen her before and as the memory returns, the tears pour down my face as I whisper, "Imogen."

Ivan steps in front of her and shakes his head. "No, Winter. This is Charlotte, Massimo's daughter."

"But…" I am so confused and then the black memory sharpens, and I see the glass coffin with the mummified remains of the woman in the painting.

"She's dead."

Alessandro grasps my hand and Angelo says with a growl, "Take her somewhere quiet. It's too much."

Alessandro pulls me to my feet, and I shout, "No!"

The word bounces from the walls, causing the room to still as I stare at the woman cowering behind Ivan.

"I want to see her."

Angelo nods and as Ivan pulls her gently forward, the tears flow as I stare at the image of the woman in the painting. I see a room. A white room. I see Massimo and I see pain. A lot of pain and fear. I whisper, "He loved her."

Nobody speaks and Charlotte looks fearful and as I stare, the image changes to the one back in the restaurant. I see the same image. Ivan and Charlotte walking hand in hand and Massimo's anger reaches out to strangle me again.

My hands fly to my throat as if he's squeezing the life out of me and I gasp, "He thought you were his wife."

Charlotte's tears match my own and she whispers, "He was wrong."

I nod and, as if a veil is lifting, everything is clear. The journey to Scarpetta. Massimo's anger and his plan to kill them all.

The entire room waits for me to speak and yet I can't as my memory starts coloring in the missing pages and as the full horror of the past two years returns to me, it brings the last puzzle piece crashing into place.

"Oh my God!" I scream so loudly it causes everyone to jump up, and as Angelo and Alessandro reach for me at the same time, I struggle to stay conscious.

I can't even speak as an agonized sound makes it out from the deepest part of my soul and I scream as the full horror hits me.

"What is it, baby?"

"Tell us, Winter. What can you see?" Angelo sounds fearful and then I drop to my knees and wrap my arms around my body as I sob, tortured cries of the damned.

Alessandro drops to his knees before me and pulls me roughly into his arms and I detect the fear in his voice as he says, "What is it? Tell us."

Lifting my grief-stricken face to his, I have only one word. "Frankie."

Then I scream, collapsing into his arms as I sob uncontrollably, my heart shredding into jagged ribbons at my feet.

"Baby, who's Frankie? Tell me."

Alessandro presses on and as I lift my eyes to his, I watch the concern change to disbelief as I whisper, "Our son."

"What the fuck?" Angelo hisses beside me and somebody screams, a woman I think, but I can't tear my eyes from my son's father as he learns of his existence for the very first time.

"Our son." The emotion in his eyes tears my heart to shreds and I sob, "We have a son. Frankie. Massimo used him to control me."

The anguish in Alessandro's eyes breaks me apart as he stares at me in utter disbelief.

Angelo says firmly, "Winter, focus. Where did Massimo place your son?"

I can't stop staring at Alessandro, who looks as broken as I am, and I whisper, "In the mansion. Locked in the nursery."

I hear more crying and the pain that is surrounding me right now is unbearable and Alessandro says sharply, his eyes never leaving mine for a second. "Tell me the place was empty when you arrived."

There is silence, and then he roars. "Tell me!"

The response appears to hover suspended in time and when it finally arrives, it drives a knife through my heart.

"There were no survivors."

For a moment, the words don't register and then as the terrible truth strikes me hard, I start screaming and nothing in the world can stop me.

CHAPTER 36

ALESSANDRO

The room erupts into confused chaos. I hold my screaming woman in my arms, her life destroyed along with mine as we face the death of our son. The son I never knew I had and as I hold her pain wrecked body, I feel numb. I have a son. I *had* a son. It's too much to comprehend and as the activity increases in the room, I can't move. I hold Winter as if I'm afraid to let go and try to wrap my head around something I never saw coming.

We have a son. Frankie.

I barely register Angelo's strong hand on my back and as the seconds turn to minutes, I am frozen to the spot. Then something kicks in, a natural instinct to protect what's mine, and I say angrily, "I want to discover where my son is."

The awkward silence is not what I need right now, and I raise my eyes to the only person I trust with this and growl, "I need to know everything."

Malik nods, looking as emotional as the rest of us, but it's not emotion I need right now, it's action.

Standing, I drag my sobbing woman to her feet and sweep her into my arms and say roughly, "We need a moment."

As I stride from the room, nobody dares stop me and as Winter weeps like a broken angel in my arms, I want answers and I want them yesterday.

* * *

Winter is inconsolable, but I have no time to waste, so I place her gently on the bed and take her hand, saying firmly, "I want you to tell me everything."

"Please, Alessandro, we must go to him."

I exhale sharply and say with the deepest pain etching my words. "I don't think you understand, Winter. There is nothing left to return to."

Her wide eyes fill with grief, and she shakes her head. "No, he must be somewhere; he must be."

Her voice breaks and I growl, "I want it all. From the moment you realized you were pregnant and every minute of my son's life. Everything you tell me is for a reason, because I refuse to accept that he is gone, and we must place ourselves in the mind of madness to work out what could have happened."

Through heart wrenching sobs, Winter tells me her harrowing story and I hang onto every word and commit it to my memory. I crave every small detail of a life I never knew existed until now. We talk for hours, and we grieve like any parents would, but I grieve for more than the son I never had. I grieve for the fact I never met him and the life we were denied because of one man.

Hours pass and I ask many questions and by the time Winter falls into an exhausted sleep, I have never experienced rage like this. I had a son and now it's my duty to step up and be the father he deserves.

Leaving Winter to sleep fitfully, I head back to the kitchen and find everyone exactly where I left them. The emotion on their faces rolls off me like water on wax because I no longer have any.

Angelo steps up and says quickly, "How is she?"

"Sleeping." I growl my response and head straight for the coffee machine. I need a clear head now and fix Jasmine with a hard look.

"Please, can you watch her?"

She jumps up. "Of course."

Louisa nods. "We'll take it in shifts. We want to help."

I note the tears streaming down Charlotte's anxious face and she says with a quiver in her voice, "I'm so sorry, it was all my fault."

Ivan hisses angrily, "None of this is your fault. There is only one man responsible for that and he's lucky he's not here right now."

Angelo shakes his head, looking as if he's been to Hell and back. "If it's anyone's fault, it's mine. We couldn't get inside, so we burned the place down. I…"

"Enough!" I round on my friends in a rage that has been brewing since hearing the news I have a son.

"We are all to blame. Nobody saw this coming. We weren't to know."

Flynn looks as destroyed as the rest of us and moves closer, saying with a gruff, "What can we do to help?"

Before I can answer, Malik's voice washes over us like a balm of antiseptic taking away the sting as he says firmly, "Take a seat. I have some information that may help."

We stare at him in surprise and waste no time in grabbing a seat at the table and he peers at his computer with a worried frown.

"As I said before, you may be interested in what I discovered, and now certain events have come to light, it begins to make sense."

There is not a sound in the room as we wait expectantly for

him to speak, and he raises his eyes to mine, and my heart quickens when I note the excitement in his.

"I hacked into Massimo's servers and found some interesting files stored on his computer. He saved them to the cloud and used a weak password to protect them." Malik shakes his head in disgust as he sighs. "They contained the usual shit, but there was one folder that interested me more than any other because it was titled with a name rather than a description."

"What was the name?" I'm guessing it's one we are all familiar with, judging from the gleam in his eye and he nods. "Ortega."

The silence says it all as I share a look with my friends around the table and understand why Malik is so excited about this. Like his own family in Dubai, the Ortegas are mafia royalty. Some consider Giovanni Ortega to be the Mafia King and I'm not surprised that Massimo had him in his sights.

"What was in the folder?" Angelo says quickly and Malik's eyes gleam.

"A series of payments set up to a woman."

"What woman?" Angelo is getting impatient, but whatever Malik has discovered is something he's excited about, and he says with a smirk, "Delores Brown."

"Should we be familiar with that name?" Flynn appears as confused as we all are, and Malik shakes his head.

"At first, I was as confused as you are. I did some more digging and found a bank account set up in Zurich for a Miss. Delores Brown. Then I cross-referenced the account numbers and payments and had a match."

"But how does this matter to us?" I huff with frustration.

"Because the payments were for services received. Once again, I did some digging on the elusive Delores Brown and discovered a birth certificate and a passport in her name."

"So, you think Delores Brown is somehow connected to Giovanni Ortega?"

"No." We stare at him in confusion as he says with rare excitement. "My sources reveal that Delores Brown was last seen leaving a party in downtown Los Angeles around a year ago. That was the last sighting of her and despite exhaustive searches, she was never found. Word is, she left the country and in the absence of a body the case remains open. It appears that whoever Delores Brown is now, is someone who doesn't want to be discovered and is hiding behind her, using her identity."

"So, how does this link to Massimo?"

Malik laughs softly. "Because at the same time the payments started, Giovanni Ortega's daughter went missing."

We all stare at Malik with more questions than answers and he grins triumphantly.

"On the day Angelo burned Massimo's house to the ground, a ticket was purchased in the name of Delores Brown to Zurich, and she wasn't traveling alone."

I stare at him with a sense of anticipation as he says triumphantly, "Her companion was a small infant listed as Benjamin Brown. I tracked the cab companies and found a booking that collected them thirty minutes after Massimo and Winter left for Scarpetta."

As the news sinks in, Malik leans back with a twisted grin on his face and says with satisfaction.

"It appears that our cuckoo fled the nest before Angelo got there, but what interests me more than anything is what connection Delores Brown has with Giovanni Ortega."

"Do you think Massimo was keeping Giovanni's daughter prisoner to bring her father down?" Ivan voices what we're all guessing and Malik shrugs. "If Delores is his daughter. She may not be."

"So, we go to Zurich."

I stand because we have no time to waste, and Malik shakes his head. "I understand your desire to find your son, Alessandro, but we need to be clever about this. If Giovanni Ortega is involved, we must tread carefully. Word is, he is tearing the world apart for news of his daughter, and we must tread in the shadows and creep up on them when they least expect it."

"But I can't just sit here."

Angelo growls, "Malik's right." He turns to me, and I hate the sympathy in his eyes as he says with a slight break to his voice. "We can't risk her going to ground. At the moment, she doesn't know we're onto her and if we race off to Zurich and tear it apart, we may never find her. The only way to deal with a mouse is the set a cat after it and we have the best one for the job."

All eyes turn to Malik, who looks almost euphoric, and I wonder if Delores Brown has just escaped one mad murdering bastard only to set herself in the path of a much more sinister one.

CHAPTER 37

WINTER

I wake from a fitful sleep to find Jasmine watching over me with concern. Almost immediately, my thoughts turn to Frankie, and I sit up with an alarmed cry.

Jasmine looks worried and says sadly, "I'm so sorry, Winter. Alessandro is with the others, working out a plan."

"A plan?" My voice shakes and she nods. "Malik has some information he was briefing them on. I'm not sure what it involved because I came to sit with you."

I don't even hesitate and head straight for the door, wrenching it open and running down the corridor, Jasmine hot on my heels. "Winter wait!"

I don't hear her and just head straight for the kitchen because I need to know that my baby is alive.

As soon as I crash through the door, Alessandro is by my side and I fall into his arms and sob, "Please, tell me my baby is alive."

I hear the emotion in his voice as he pulls away and stares deep into my eyes. "Malik has some information that points to a woman leaving just after you with a young baby."

My eyes widen in hope and just seeing the emotion in his eyes makes the tears flow rapidly down my face unchecked.

"Frankie?" I whisper, not really daring to hope it was him and Alessandro nods, his voice breaking a little as he whispers, "It's complicated, but we must trust Malik to bring our son home."

My head jerks to Malik, who is watching with glittering emotion in his usual expressionless eyes, and I say falteringly, "Malik."

He nods and says smoothly, "I leave in an hour."

"I want to come."

I hate that he shakes his head, appearing upset, and Angelo moves to my side and says in his deep, authoritative voice, "Let Malik do his job, Winter."

"No, I want to go!" I almost scream at him, and he says angrily, "Don't you think I know how you feel? When you were taken from us, I wanted to tear Massimo apart with my bare hands. I thought it would be easy to storm into his home and drag you away from him and if I had given into my emotion, none of us would be here now, Frankie included."

His words hit me hard across the face and the pain in his eyes mirrors my own as I sob, "But I'm his mother and my place is with my baby."

Angelo pulls me roughly into his arms and whispers, "We will bring him back to you. Trust Malik and trust me. The best thing you can do is wait, no matter how hard that will be, and as soon as Malik has Frankie, you and Alessandro will be the first people he sees."

Wrenching away from my twin, I stumble across the room to Malik and, staring into his eyes, whisper, "Bring him back to me, Malik. Be the demon you are and don't leave anything to chance. Frankie is our family, and he needs to be here."

Malik nods and, leaning in, whispers, "I will not fail you, Winter. You have my word."

As he pulls back, I shiver at the gleam in his eye that tells me whoever has my baby had better start running because being on the end of Malik's leash will make for an extremely painful walk on the wild side.

* * *

We watch Malik leave, wasting no time in organizing his trip and as I sit in the kitchen staring into a mug of coffee, Charlotte drops into the seat beside me and says tentatively, "I'm so sorry, Winter, it's as if I'm responsible somehow."

Looking up, I register her tear-stained cheeks and red-rimmed eyes and yet despite it all, she is the image of sweet innocence, much like her mother was. Thinking of the terrible fate that awaited her if Massimo had his wish, if anything, I'm proud to have prevented that from happening and to her surprise, along with mine, I pull her close and whisper, "I can never hate you. Your father was mad with grief and his mind was twisted and he lost touch with reality a long time ago. Don't you dare mourn for something that would have destroyed you in the end and know you are better off not knowing what he had planned for your future."

She sobs on my shoulder as I hold her like a baby and whispers, "You are as strong as they said you were. I'm so happy they brought you home."

As we cling together, I experience nothing but love for Ivan's wife. She is innocent in all this. She had her part to play in bringing me home, and I could never hate her just because of who her father is.

As we pull back, I note Louisa's concerned expression across the table, and I smile tentatively. "So, here we are, a club of our own, I guess."

Louisa nods. "Club Mafia Wives, I'm guessing."

Jasmine grins. "God help us."

We all look up and note our men talking in hushed whispers by the glass doors leading into the garden and Jasmine sighs. "We must stick together."

Louisa nods vigorously. "It won't be easy."

Charlotte brushes a tear from her eye and stares at Ivan with undisguised longing. "They're rather hot, though."

It has the desired effect and as we all share a look, it's one of solidarity because we are no longer outnumbered. We have a purpose, and it appears that the wives of Club Mafia will play a very important role in the future that begins when I get my son back.

* * *

AFTER WHAT FEELS LIKE HOURS, Alessandro heads to my side and I fall against him, loving how his arm wraps around me in protective love, keeping me safe.

The others drifted off to their respective husbands and I whisper, "I'm sorry, Alessandro."

He plays with my hair, twisting it through his fingers and letting it fall.

"I hate that I couldn't remember Frankie. What sort of mother does that make me?"

"You are the best mother he could wish for, baby." His low growl reassures me a little as he says with husky emotion, "You survived to bring him back to me. You suffered unimaginable horror just to keep him safe, and you endured the greatest hardship because of him."

"Will everything be ok?" I am so anxious about that, and he grips my face hard between his hands and stares fiercely into my eyes. "Malik will bring him back to us. I don't doubt that for a second, and then when we are a family, I will make you my wife."

"But your grandfather…"

"Will accept it. You see baby, my grandfather places family above everything and when he learns I have a son, all deals are off. You and Frankie are my family, and that will never change. I'm not my grandfather. I don't want anyone else—ever. It's all about you, Winter, it always has been, and now that includes our son. We have a chance at a fresh start that I never believed was possible and I will fight to the death to protect you both along with the many brothers and sisters I have planned for Frankie."

"Many?" I stare at him in shock, and he grins wickedly, "You better believe it, baby because I intend to create many mirror images of us both and I will love every second of it."

His lips claim mine in a sweet, deep, soul shattering kiss and despite the ache in both our hearts, at least we are together. A vital piece of us is missing but we have faith in Malik to bring our son back to us and so, as we drift off to bed, I want to spend the entire time Frankie is away, wrapped in Alessandro's protective arms.

CHAPTER 38

MASSIMO

The rage burns deep inside as I am transported like an animal in a crate to Los Angeles. Winter has overstepped the mark; she will pay dearly for this.

As the poison seeped through my system, my body shut down, locking me in a prison that I will never escape from.

Imogen betrayed me. She married a Russian and they are laughing at me. Always laughing at me. I saw the amusement on their faces as they stood before me, hand in hand and I will never recover from the sight of my wife touching another man.

Images of them fucking in my bed are haunting me and there is nothing I can do about it.

All I can do is imagine what I will do to them when the doctors find a cure for this devastating condition Winter inflicted on me.

She is no better. Openly kissing her lover before me, tainting my beautiful doll. It appears she lost her memory. That's something at least. Maybe she will never remember she has a son.

The regret deepens when I think about the perfect human created for my pleasure. He will never receive my love. Never experience what it's like to be the object of my affection. I had such a promising future planned for us both. He would fall in love with me. We would be happy.

The aircraft lands and the medics enter, grabbing the handles of my wheelchair and saying in excruciating cheerful voices, "Here he is. Not long now and we'll have you safely home where you belong."

Home! For a moment, I imagine they have found a cure. I will be free. I will get my revenge on them all and make their pain and suffering last a lifetime.

My heart lifts at the thought of being released from my prison and as I'm pushed down a ramp into a waiting ambulance, I almost expect the driver to head to my mansion.

I will instruct my men to round up my enemies. To bring them to my dungeons, where I will have them dismembered before my eyes. My loyal servants will do whatever I ask. I will reign supreme, and everything will be just as I had planned.

All of them. The men who brought me down and the women who let them. My darling Imogen will laugh and clap her hands in delight when I spill the Russian's organs from his body and serve them to her to dine on and drink his blood. They will all pay. I will make certain of that. Portia, Don Majerio, and his bastard grandson. Winter and her brother, Angelo. Louisa and her husband who played their part in this. They will all suffer because I am the most astute player in the game. I am Massimo Delauren, and nothing will ever bring me down.

When the ambulance stops, I imagine seeing the familiar façade of my home. What I see is very different.

I know this place.

The screaming starts in my head but remains there because I have no outlet to release it. They must be wrong. I don't belong here. Not here–anywhere but here.

As I'm pushed down the familiar sterile corridors, I pray that I'm not heading where I think I am, but as we take the usual elevator and spill out into the long white corridor, I understand exactly what they have planned.

"Here you go, Massimo buddy. We've found you a place next to a familiar face."

As the door opens those malevolent eyes glare at me from her position by the window. Disapproving, chilling and disappointed. Always disappointed in me and I can almost feel the pain when she slapped me around the ears and caned me into submission.

I want to run, I want to leave, I want to be anywhere but here with her. She will ruin me, destroy me and she will make my life hell just like she did all those years ago.

"I know, I'll position you facing one another, won't that be lovely?"

The cheery nurse says with false optimism.

As I come eye to eye with the woman who drove me to a chilling place in my head, I cower before her angry gaze and the panic wraps me in bitterness and fear as my nanny, Iris Young, stares malevolently into my eyes.

Somehow, through the madness, I see them all laughing at me. My father, my mother and my brother. Every single person I have ever met has played a part in this madness and as I face the rest of my days staring into the sadistic eyes of the one I fear the most, I suffer the crushing realization of defeat.

EPILOGUE

MALIK

The small house set in a suburban street looks so normal it brings a rare smile to my face. If the neighbors knew who was hiding inside, they would lock their doors and wait for the storm to pass. I note them going about their daily chores, living the kind of life I could never imagine.

A dog barks and I hear a baby cry and my ears prick up as I sense my journey may be over before it's even begun.

"Everyone is in place, sir."

Ali, my trusted soldier, growls from his position beside me and I dust an imaginary speck of dust from my lap.

As I stare at the front door with interest, I'm surprised when it opens and a young woman steps out, looking around her with a guarded expression, almost as if she knows what's about to happen.

"Do you want us to strike, sir?"

Ali sounds as if we're out for a stroll in the park and, as always, nothing troubles him.

I hold up my hand and say smoothly, "Wait."

As the woman begins jogging along the street, I say in a

deep voice, "Instruct the soldiers to enter the house. Search the rooms and report back."

Ali talks into his phone and when he finishes, I say darkly, "We follow her."

As the car pulls off from the curb, we watch her disappear around the corner. Delores Brown. At least that's the name on the rental agreement, and yet she is an imposter. The fact she's alone tells me this won't be as straightforward as I hoped and as Ali takes the call, he sighs. "Empty."

"Search for any evidence."

I stare as the woman jogs in the distance, admiring her ass as she sways from side to side. Her long dark hair is tied in a topknot that releases a few strands that trail against her creamy white neck.

"Nothing, sir." Ali huffs with disappointment and my eyes narrow.

"Take me back to the house."

"But the woman…"

"Is going nowhere. She'll return and we'll be waiting for her."

As we head back to the house, we park outside, and the door flies open, allowing me to step into the sunshine.

As I sniff the air, I detect the distressing scent of suburbia that is at odds with the way I live my life.

My soldiers open the door and allow me to enter a space that has me glancing around with derision. Do people really live like this? This entire house would fit into my shoe closet, and I feel an urgent need to return to the clean air of wealth and privilege.

I wander through the rooms and see living at its most basic. Only practical items are in situ and as I prowl into the bedroom, I am disappointed to note no evidence of any child living here. There are two bedrooms in total and both are clean and free from personal objects, only an open bag on the side revealing the person is not here for long.

On opening the closet, I see a few garments on hangers and wrinkle my nose in disgust. Then I head to the bathroom and breathe in the aroma of products that are definitely not from the shelves of the high-end stores I have accounts with.

Ali hovers by the door and I say roughly, "Wait in the car. When she arrives, cover the exits. We will be taking her hostage."

"Usual way?"

"Of course."

Ali nods and retreats to the waiting car and as I take my seat in the wooden chair placed behind the door, I stare out of the window, relishing the anticipation of an interrogation that will be most pleasurable.

I wait for forty minutes and then hear the door slam and the heavy breathing of a woman who has pushed herself to her limits. How I adore limits. How I love breaking them and testing my subject to reach new ones.

As the door opens into the bedroom, she doesn't see me as she strips off her sweat-soaked running vest and shrugs out of her jogging pants. I take a moment to admire a body I am keen to explore further and as she loosens her hair from the top knot, my cock wakes up and takes an interest.

To distract it, I slam the door shut and as she jumps and looks around, her scream washes through my body like the finest champagne.

"What the fuck!"

She attempts to cover her naked body and I growl, "Take a seat, Miss. Brown."

Her eyes widen and she appears to have lost the power of speech as she drops to the bed and pulls the comforter around her body.

"Who are you?" She says with a low hiss, and I grin, my eyes flashing as I growl, "Your worst nightmare."

I said, "Who are you?"

I admire her anger and revel in it for a second and then I shrug. "That is no concern of yours. I want the baby you stole from Massimo Delauren."

Her eyes widen and her lip trembles and she appears so afraid I take a moment to enjoy the sight.

"He sent you?" She looks as if she's about to hurl and I play along, feasting on her fear. "Sort of."

Her eyes flicker around the room, almost as if she expects the man himself to appear and I stand and love the fear darken her eyes as I prowl toward her. As I grasp her hair in my fist, I lean down and growl, "Where is he?"

"What are you talking about?"

She fires back and the hate sparkling in her eyes gives me an instant hard-on.

As I twist her hair tighter, I relish the tears that spring to her eyes and I growl, "Then you had better remember, and fast."

Pulling sharply down, I take a moment to enjoy her fear and then she surprises me by saying through gritted teeth, "Let me go, you fucking deranged bastard. You've got the wrong person."

I stare deep into her eyes and hiss. "Then you leave me no choice."

Before she can even take a breath to answer me, I press two fingers hard against her neck and as she slumps in my arms, I take a moment to enjoy the high that always gives me. To control another person's body against their will seriously turns me on and as I glance down at the beautiful lady in my arms, dressed in nothing but startled surprise, I am very much looking forward to interrogating this mafia princess because I am in no doubt at all that Delores Brown's real name is Eliza

Ortega and knowing that family, this will be an extremely interesting battle ahead.

Thank you for reading Club Mafia–The Beast
The next book in the series is
Club Mafia – The Demon

If you want to know what happened at Rockwell Academy read
Club Mafia–The Contract.

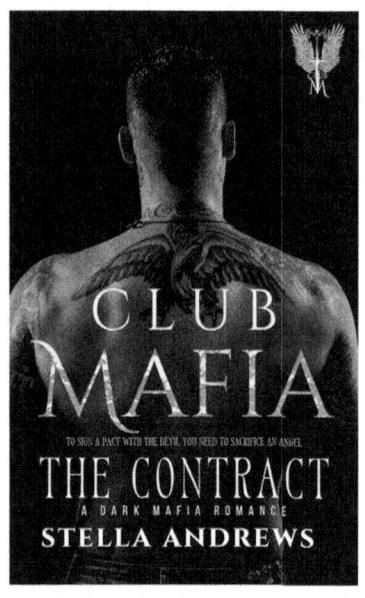

Read the entire series
Club Mafia

Thank you for reading this story.
If you have enjoyed the fantasy world of this novel, please would you be so kind as to leave a review on Amazon?

Join my closed Facebook Group

Stella's Sexy Readers

Follow me on Instagram

Carry on reading for more Reaper Romances, Mafia Romance & more.
Remember to grab your free book by visiting stellaandrews.com.

ALSO BY STELLA ANDREWS

Twisted Reapers

Sealed With a Broken Kiss
Dirty Hero (Snake & Bonnie)
Daddy's Girls (Ryder & Ashton)
Twisted (Sam & Kitty)
The Billion Dollar baby (Tyler & Sydney)
Bodyguard (Jet & Lucy)
Flash (Flash & Jennifer)
Country Girl (Tyson & Sunny)

The Romanos
The Throne of Pain (Lucian & Riley)
The Throne of Hate (Dante & Isabella)
The Throne of Fear (Romeo & Ivy)
Lorenzo's story is in Broken Beauty

Beauty Series
Breaking Beauty (Sebastian & Angel) *
Owning Beauty (Tobias & Anastasia)
Broken Beauty (Maverick & Sophia) *
Completing Beauty – The series

Five Kings
Catch a King (Sawyer & Millie) *
Slade

Steal a King

Break a King

Destroy a King

Marry a King

Baron

Club Mafia

Club Mafia – The Contract

Club Mafia – The Boss

Club Mafia – The Angel

Club Mafia – The Savage

Club Mafia - The Beast

Club Mafia – The Demon

Standalone

The Highest Bidder (Logan & Samantha)

Rocked (Jax & Emily)

Brutally British

Deck the Boss

Reasons to sign up to my mailing list.

•A reminder that you can read my books FREE with Kindle Unlimited.

•Receive a monthly newsletter so you don't miss out on any special offers or new releases.

•Links to follow me on Amazon or social media to be kept up to date with new releases.

•Free books and bonus content.

•Opportunities to read my books before they are even released by joining my team.

•Sneak peeks at new material before anyone else.

stellaandrews.com

Follow me on Amazon

Printed in Great Britain
by Amazon